"So, you can't face working here now that Longman is gone?"

Matthew Canning leaned back in his chair, his eyes cold.

"That's outrageous!" Ellis glared at him.

He shrugged. "Your first glimpse of what it would be like to work for me put you off completely, didn't it?"

"Certainly not. It wasn't the work that made me change my mind," she assured him bitingly. "It was the nature of it. I dislike the thought of never working on my own initiative. And," she added, "it seemed to me that rubbing along together, as you put it, would not only be difficult, but downright impossible."

Matthew regarded her briefly. "To hark back to a recent conversation of ours, you don't understand me, either, Miss Worth. I never resist a challenge." And, holding her eyes very deliberately, he tore up her resignation and threw the pieces in his wastepaper basket....

Catherine George was born in Wales and, following her marriage to an engineer, lived in Brazil for eight years at a gold-mine site. It was an experience she would later draw upon for her books, when she and her husband returned to England. Now her husband helps manage their household so that Catherine can devote more time to her writing. They have two children—a daughter and a son— who share their mother's love of language and writing.

Books by Catherine George

HARLEQUIN ROMANCE

2942—THIS TIME ROUND
3081—CONSOLATION PRIZE
3129—ARROGANT INTERLOPER
3147—A CIVILISED ARRANGEMENT
3177—UNLIKELY CUPID
3201—BRAZILIAN ENCHANTMENT

HARLEQUIN PRESENTS

1016—LOVE LIES SLEEPING
1065—TOUCH ME IN THE MORNING
1152—VILLAIN OF THE PIECE
1184—TRUE PARADISE
1225—LOVEKNOT
1255—EVER SINCE EDEN
1321—COME BACK TO ME

LEADER OF THE PACK
Catherine George

Harlequin Books

TORONTO • NEW YORK • LONDON
AMSTERDAM • PARIS • SYDNEY • HAMBURG
STOCKHOLM • ATHENS • TOKYO • MILAN
MADRID • WARSAW • BUDAPEST • AUCKLAND

Original hardcover edition published in 1991
by Mills & Boon Limited

ISBN 0-373-03236-6

Harlequin Romance first edition December 1992

LEADER OF THE PACK

CHAPTER ONE

ELLIS liked to arrive long before the rest of the work-force. Today, of all days, someone had beaten her to it. A strange car occupied one of the spaces marked 'Visitors'. Its driver leaned against his gleaming black Lotus, his face hidden behind the pink pages of the *Financial Times* in total absorption. But as she drew level with him he lowered his newspaper suddenly, revealing an aquiline face under thick straight hair which shone in the early sunlight like her aunt's mahogany dining table.

Ellis acknowledged his greeting with a cool little nod, then continued on her way towards the office building, rather amused when the stranger, unaware that she could see his reflection in the glass doors of the entrance, watched her out of sight.

She speculated, intrigued, on who he could be. She'd worked long enough for the company to know most people who came and went at Colcraft Holdings. This man was new to her, and definitely not someone to see Charles—Mr Longman. Like any secretary worth her salt, she had all *his* appointments off by heart for the foreseeable future, and there were no unknown quantities on the list.

At the thought of Charles Longman, Ellis forgot the impressive stranger in a surge of excitement. Charles had been looking forward to this day of days for a very long time. And so had she. Even the weather was perfect. The June sun was shining, the sky cloudless, and Ellis herself festive in a new suit bought for the occasion.

The foyer was deserted at this hour, with no receptionist in her bower of telephones and greenery. There was an air of hushed expectancy about the building, as always at this time of day, as if it waited, impatient, for the humans who brought it to life. Ellis sighed with satisfaction as she pressed the button for the lift. She loved this early morning period when she had the entire building to herself—loved every last thing about her job if it came to that. Few women had the good fortune to enjoy their work as much as she did.

When Ellis left the lift on the top floor she lingered a little, admiring the view from the windows which lined the corridor of Colcraft power. The spa town of Pennington gleamed today in the sunshine, the flowerbeds in the tree-lined square below a blaze of colour. Almost, thought Ellis, as though the town were joining in the celebration.

In her orderly office she hung up her jacket, tucked her white silk shirt neatly in place, then ran a comb through her bright brown hair, which fell in glossy layers across her forehead in a short, skilled cut she regarded as her main extravagance. She checked her straight nose for shine, added a touch of discreet colour to the curves of a mouth she considered too full for a brighter shade. Lastly she put on the tinted spectacles necessary to combat eye-strain from various computer screens, then checked on the diary for the events of the day.

At last she allowed herself to go through the communicating door into the office of Charles Longman, sales director. She stopped dead in the doorway, astonished to find him already there, standing tall and still at the window. Unlike every other morning Charles Longman was, amazingly, in his office before her. He stood with his back to her, oblivious of her presence, gazing down at the square below with such absorption that an onlooker might have thought he was seeing it for the first time.

Ellis stiffened. Sensitive as always to every nuance of Charles Longman's moods, she knew at once that something was wrong. She coughed slightly to attract his attention.

'Good morning, Mr Longman. I didn't see your car when I arrived.'

Charles Longman turned slowly to face the trim, attractive figure in the doorway.

'Ellis?' His eyes looked blank, as though he had difficulty in recognising her. 'Oh—yes. I dropped the car at the garage for a service on the way in. You're very early today.'

She smiled faintly. 'Not really, Mr Longman. It's the normal hour for me. *You're* the early bird today.'

The bitterness of his answering smile matched the look in his blue eyes, which, Ellis saw as she moved closer, were bloodshot, with dark marks beneath them.

'Early bird I may be,' he said, a catch in the drawling voice which normally oozed self-confidence, 'but I failed to catch the worm after all, Ellis.'

Her eyes widened incredulously. '*What?* You don't mean . . .?'

Charles nodded, his mouth still in the meaningless rictus of a smile. 'Called I might have been, chosen I was not.'

The silence following his announcement was painful.

Ellis stared at him, dumbfounded, unable to take in what Charles had said, certain there must be some mistake. She pulled herself together.

'I'll make some coffee,' she said briskly. 'Then while you drink it perhaps you'll tell me what went wrong. Unless it's confidential, of course.'

Charles sighed, slumping down in the chair behind his desk. 'What do I ever keep from you, Ellis? Of course I'll tell you what happened. Lord knows you're likely to be more sympathetic than Clissy.'

So Mrs Longman hadn't taken kindly to the news. Ellis, who fought a constant battle with her dislike of Clarissa Longman, tried to quell her animosity as she made strong black coffee and set Spode cups on a silver tray. When she carried it in she found Charles with his head in his hands, every line of his graceful body eloquent with defeat.

Ellis handed him a cup of black, sweet coffee, then sat down in her usual place in front of the desk to drink her own.

'Did you dine with Mr Maitland last night as arranged?' she asked at last, since Charles seemed disinclined to break the silence.

'Oh, yes.' His smile was crooked. 'We dined, we talked, we drank some vintage port, smoked a couple of superb cigars. Then, when I was feeling absolutely on top of the world and certain what he'd say next, Oliver Maitland looked me in the eye and delivered the *coup de grâce*. He's abdicating his throne, right enough, almost immediately, in fact, but...' He paused, biting his lip until he drew blood. '*But*, Ellis,

I made a bloody great mistake in assuming I was the automatic heir apparent.'

'But why?' she demanded fiercely. 'Surely it was a foregone conclusion? Everyone thought...'

'Everyone thought wrong. You and me included.' Charles flashed the meaningless smile at her again. 'Despite my impeccable education, not to mention my family connections, Miss Worth, dear, I was told— and this is for your ears only—that, happy though my reign as sales director of Colcraft Holdings may have been, it was nowhere near as glorious as required. Don't look so shattered; I'm not getting the push, exactly, more a sideways nudge. I shall even rejoice in the title of managing director, Ellis, but of only one solitary subsidiary company, one of the many beneath our Colcraft umbrella. The new post is considered more in keeping with my particular talents. Or lack of same,' he added bitterly.

Ellis felt the blood draining from her cheeks. 'Where?' she asked huskily.

'Not very far away, oddly enough!' With sudden violence Charles swivelled round in his chair and hurled his empty coffee-cup at the wall. Then, as if nothing had happened, he told Ellis that his wife wouldn't even have to give up the house and stables. He was to head up CCS Energy Conservation Systems, a company well within travelling distance of his home. 'And because I'm saddled—if you'll pardon the pun,' he said wryly, 'with a wife who spends a fortune on her blasted horses, I shall just have to buckle down and do my best to earn my daily bread, which, though not buttered in quite the same manner as it would have been as MD of Colcraft, will be a definite improvement on the present arrangement.'

Ellis soon learned why Charles Longman had turned up so singularly early for once. He, along with several colleagues at the same level, was bidden to the boardroom for a meeting with the retiring managing director.

When he'd gone Ellis gathered up the broken shards of what had once been a quite valuable cup, then returned to her own office to carry on as usual. Almost as if, she thought drearily, it were any other day, instead of one of the blackest of her life. As she worked swiftly, as usual, her mind functioned at even greater speed. Charles had made no mention of her own fate. Now he was leaving, who would take over his job? Because if, as was company policy, it was someone within the organisation, the new sales director would naturally prefer to keep his own secretary. Which left Ellis Worth out in the cold.

In contrast to the June sunshine outside, Ellis's mood was arctic. It wasn't, she thought with pain, as if she were just losing an employer. Since her very first day as Charles's secretary her feelings for him had been far warmer than anyone guessed. Awake to all his faults, with no illusions about his weaknesses, she'd been hopelessly in love with him for years. But Ellis, brought up to have strong views on the sanctity of marriage, had hidden her secret well, from Charles most of all. If he'd ever shown the least sign of reciprocating her feelings she would have resigned at once. The role of the 'other woman' was not for her. Ever. And it was all Charles Longman had to offer. She knew for certain he'd never leave his well-connected Clarissa, even though it was well known that the lady paid more attention to her horses than her husband.

The full curves of Ellis's mouth took on a downward, bitter droop. She wasn't the first woman to nourish a secret passion for her boss, of course—it was, after all, the cliché of clichés. She was, she told herself firmly, grateful to fate for arranging to remove Charles from her life. Which sensible conclusion did little to soothe her pain at the prospect of never seeing him again once he took up his new post. Her gloom was so absolute that she jumped yards when a slim hand adorned with a familiar gold signet ring fell on her shoulder.

'Steady on, Ellis,' drawled Charles, his blue eyes amused as she leapt to her feet. 'Come into my office and bring some coffee again—I promise not to decorate the wall with it this time.'

Once they were seated on opposite sides of the desk, Ellis eyed Charles Longman closely, rather surprised to see that he looked very much more like himself, no longer the defeated man of earlier on.

'Am I allowed to ask who's taking over from Mr Maitland?' she asked.

Charles gave her a caustic smile. 'An old chum of my wife's, as it happens. Chap by the name of Matthew Canning. You've probably heard of him.'

Ellis thought for a moment. 'You mean the man who's supposed to be something of a miracle worker?'

'That's the one. You can't blame the Board, I suppose. If a man can take a couple of companies by the throat one after another and turn them over from failure in record time it's only natural he'll rise to the very top. The cream, dear Ellis, always does.'

The Board, it seemed, had been unanimous in voting Matthew Canning the best man to take charge of Colcraft, which was a holding company with a large group of subsidiaries engaged in activities varying from the production of textiles and lighting to building supplies and property development.

'Doesn't matter a toss what the firm actually does,' said Charles. 'Canning's got the knack of turning it over from loss to profitability like lightning. A powerhouse of a chap. I met him again just now.'

'He's here *already*?'

'Maitland thought it best to introduce him to his merry crew at the first opportunity.' Charles sighed. 'Do you know, Ellis, that I'm forty-two next week?'

'Of course I do.'

'This chap is years younger than me, would you believe? Makes me feel bloody ancient, fit for nothing but the scrap-heap.'

Not to me, thought Ellis with hidden passion, her eyes unguarded for an instant. Charles, too deep in his own depression to notice, went on to inform her that the new man would be in need of a secretary, because Oliver Maitland's terrifying Miss Morrison would be retiring with him.

Ellis waited expectantly, but Charles merely went on to say that Maitland intended leaving at once now Matthew Canning's succession to his throne was confirmed.

'The old boy can't wait to get away.' Charles looked morose. 'Dan Hennessy's taking over my job, by the way. My esteemed second-in-command has been breathing down my neck for a while now, so I suppose it's no surprise. He's a very able chap.' He pulled a face. 'And tomorrow evening, God help us all, Maitland's throwing a party in the boardroom for all the heads of staff and their consorts, by way of a farewell party.'

Doesn't anyone care what happens to me? thought Ellis despairingly as she went back to her office. Dan Hennessy already had a highly efficient secretary of his own, her friend, Vicky Fisher. Which meant, it seemed, that if Ellis Worth wanted to stay at Colcraft she had no choice but to apply for the job of secretary to the new managing director, along with all the other hopefuls who'd be falling over themselves to do the same the moment the job went up for grabs.

Colcraft management enjoyed the privilege of a private dining-room, but the rest of the staff lunched in the basement cafeteria provided for the purpose. Ellis's lunchbreak that day was a nightmare. She spent the entire time fielding a barrage of questions from all sides. The news, she found, was already out about Miss Morrison's retirement. Speculation about the vacant post was intense.

'What about you?' asked Vicky Fisher. 'Will you apply, Ellis?'

'No.'

Vicky looked dejected. 'Oh, lord, I was so afraid of that. I feel terrible! I mean, here I am getting a sort of promotion now Mr Hennessy's to be sales director, but I never dreamed I'd be putting *you* out of a job. I thought you'd be moved up to MD's secretary automatically.'

Ellis smiled wryly. 'Like part of the office furniture.'

'No! I mean because you're so highly qualified, and, well, dedicated. Nobody else here has slaved away to better themselves like you.'

Ellis knew this was true enough. Part of her devotion to Charles stemmed from his encouragement of her part-time studies with the Chartered Institute of Secretaries and Administrators. It had taken years of sheer grind, but she'd been qualified now for more than a year. Not that it had made any difference to her salary or her job, other than her ability to shoulder more and more of Charles Longman's burden.

'I'll start looking in the appointments section of the newspapers, or maybe register with one of those postfinder bureaux. There's bound to be an opening somewhere.'

'Especially now you've got letters after your name,' added Vicky reassuringly.

Ellis, utterly jaded after her trying lunch-hour, returned to her office with rather less than her usual zest for work. Charles buzzed her almost as soon as she arrived.

'Unlike you to be late back from lunch,' he commented.

'I didn't *get* any lunch worth mentioning. Everyone kept firing questions at me about the reshuffle. It was like question time in the House.'

Charles's smile was perfunctory. 'A note for the diary, Ellis. Canning wants the morning kept free for an informal meeting with me—*and*,' he added significantly, 'he wants you there, too.'

'*Me?* Why?'

'I think Oliver Maitland's description of you whetted his curiosity.'

'What did Mr Maitland say?'

'Told Canning my Miss Worth was worth her weight in gold!'

'How droll,' said Ellis, unamused.

'Don't be angry.' Charles smiled at her placatingly. 'I agreed with him, Ellis—lord knows it's the absolute truth.' He came swiftly round the desk, astonishing her by taking her hands in his and squeezing them. 'We've been together a long time, Ellis, you and I. How the hell will I manage without you in the new place?'

Unused to physical demonstrations of any kind from Charles Longman, Ellis stood rooted to the spot in surprise. 'No one's indispensable,' she said gruffly.

'Some a great deal more than others, Ellis.' His eyes gleamed, suddenly intent as he looked down into hers. 'Will you miss me?'

'Of course.' Ellis's heart gave a giant thump in her chest as Charles bent suddenly and kissed her square on the mouth, only to leap away with a muffled curse as a knock on the door interrupted them.

Ellis envied Charles his unruffled *bonhomie* as he turned, smiling, to greet the man she recognised with a sinking heart as the stranger last seen leaning against his Lotus in the car park.

'Come in, come in, old chap,' said Charles jovially, apparently not in the least put out at being discovered mid-embrace with his secretary. 'I was just telling Ellis here you'd like a meeting with both of us in the morning.'

Ellis would have sold her soul to escape, to put her office door between herself and the man who advanced with outstretched hand as Charles made the necessary introductions. Instead she stood her ground, her colour high, very much aware that from the look in the newcomer's eyes he'd put the worst possible construction on the episode.

'How do you do, Miss Worth?' said Matthew Canning, in a voice half an octave deeper than the drawling tones of Charles Longman. At the sound of it every hair in Ellis's spine rose up in revolt as she met the cold, appraising eyes of the new man at the top.

'How do you do, Mr Canning?' she said with composure, then glanced at Charles. 'I've a lot to do. If you don't need me . . .'

'Of course, Ellis. You get on.' Charles smiled, unembarrassed, as he held the door for her, and with head high Ellis beat a reasonably dignified retreat into her own office.

So, she thought, as her fingers danced over her keyboard. That was the new *wunderkind* himself. What a way to meet him. Fate really had it in for her one way and another at this particular moment in time. Her eyes narrowed. Matthew Canning might well be younger than Charles, but street-wise she'd take bets he was way ahead of him. His timing alone was fantastic. Why, oh, why had he taken it into his head to materialise at that particular moment? Ellis ground her teeth impotently. There had been no time to register the kiss even. Before she'd known what was happening Charles had been shying away like a startled horse, and any reaction she might have felt was swamped in an agony of embarrassment at being caught in what Matthew Canning would never believe was a totally innocent act.

Ellis paused, her fingers stilled on the keys. The incident put paid once and for all to any idea of applying for the job of secretary to the new managing director. It was, she knew perfectly well, what everyone expected her to do, Charles included, probably. Not, she reflected, sighing, that so far he'd made any mention of her own future, or expressed the slightest concern over it, which was no surprise. Years of working for Charles had inured her to his many shortcomings. At the same time, unfortunately, those years together had also managed to spoil her for working for anyone else. The days would be dull without the charm of the attractive Mr Longman. Not, Ellis admitted honestly, that Matthew Canning was exactly a non-runner in the attraction stakes. He might not be dark and suave like Charles, but he was undeniably taller, with a muscular, tough aura to him which Charles quite definitely lacked. Matthew Canning's hand when he'd shaken hers had been large and hard and ringless, and slightly rough to the touch. And the eyes bright with such unconcealed distaste had been grey, not blue, with smoke-rings of darker grey rimming the lucent irises.

She shrugged impatiently. Matthew Canning's opinion of her was an irrelevance. Nevertheless she couldn't help wondering how long he'd been standing there, a witness to that intimate but totally innocent token of parting between herself and Charles. Not that it mattered. She'd be gone from Colcraft as soon as she could possibly arrange it. She couldn't bear the thought of staying on the scene to watch Matthew Canning usurping Charles Longman's rightful role, as ruler of the Colcraft roost.

Deciding she'd wasted far too much time in brooding, Ellis put both men firmly from her mind as she made determined inroads on her day's work to the constant accompaniment of the telephone as she dealt with queries from one or other of the subsidiary companies. Lately Ellis had grown accustomed to solving a large percentage of routine problems without troubling Charles Longman. Over and above her qualifications and experience, she had the good fortune to possess a memory stored with such an enormous quantity of data that she rarely needed recourse to files and records, an asset Charles found invaluable.

She was absorbed in conversation with the surveyor of one of the property developers under Colcraft's aegis when a knock on the door interrupted her discussion on solutions to a problem with the new shopping centre under construction on the outskirts of Pennington.

'Come in,' she called absently, still deep in facts and figures, then glanced up, unpleasantly surprised to see Matthew Canning. She went on with her conversation, steeling herself to remain impassive as he watched, but after a minute or two she put an end to the discussion, promising the development surveyor more detailed information next day.

Ellis found it was a definite advantage to face Matthew Canning across the bastion of her own desk. She smiled politely.

'Won't you sit down, Mr Canning?'

'Thank you.' He took the chair she indicated, and sat, relaxed, looking about him at the spick-and-span order of the room. 'I couldn't help overhearing. You carry quite an armoury of facts in your head, Miss Worth.'

'They say the human mind is a better computer than any machine invented by man.'

'I'm impressed. The man on the line must have been too.'

Ellis shrugged. 'The development surveyor of Spa Properties is a woman, Mr Canning. She gives constantly of her best, and expects the same from me as a matter of course.'

'I stand—or rather sit—corrected,' he said wryly, then put an end to pleasantries. 'Miss Worth, I'm here to discuss the question of the vacant secretarial post. Frankly I would have thought secretary to the managing director merited the job description of PA, but I gather the term is frowned on here at headquarters.'

Ellis nodded. 'Not even Miss Morrison, who was with Mr Maitland for twenty years, ever attained such heights, Mr Canning.'

'Then let's keep to the status quo. At least for the time being.' His remarkable eyes, unnerving at such close quarters, locked with hers. 'I'm here to ask whether you intend to apply.'

So you can tell me not to bother I suppose, thought Ellis bitterly. 'No, Mr Canning,' she said out loud. 'I don't.'

'May I ask why not?'

'Personal reasons.' Ellis shuffled the papers in front of her pointedly. 'If that's all, Mr Canning——'

'You've got something else lined up?' he said swiftly.

What she would have given to say yes! 'No. Not yet. But my qualifications are good; I have years of experience here at Colcraft—I should find something without too much trouble.'

'I'm sure you will.' He leaned back in his chair. 'But it might take longer than you want. So why not work for me in the meantime for, say, three months or so? I'll be frank. It would be a great help as far as I'm concerned to start off with a secretary of your skill and experience. But it would also be to your advantage, give you more time to find exactly the right job.'

Ellis looked at him thoughtfully, secretly taken very much aback by his suggestion. After he'd surprised her mid-embrace with Charles she would have put herself last on the secretarial list where Matthew Canning was concerned. Not that she had the slightest intention of looking a gift horse in the mouth. It was far too sensible a solution to her problem.

'So much seems to have happened all at once today that I can't really give you an answer off the top of my head, Mr Canning,' she said at last. 'May I have time to think it over?'

'Of course.' He rose to his feet. 'But let me know first thing in the morning, in case I have to set wheels in motion to find someone else.' He paused in the doorway. 'But after Longman leaves on Friday you'll be at a loose end anyway. It seems only practical to work for me pro tem.' He nodded courteously, then closed the door behind him, leaving Ellis to sag in her chair like a pricked balloon.

Friday! She had never imagined for a moment that Charles would leave so soon. She was shattered to realise that after this week she might never see him again. Resisting the urge to lay her head down on her desk and howl like a baby, Ellis resumed her interrupted routine with iron determination. A bitter little smile played at the corners of her mouth as she worked. Odd, she reflected, that the one who'd spared a thought for her future was Matthew Canning after all, not Charles Longman.

CHAPTER TWO

ELLIS arrived home late, drained and exhausted, more grateful than ever before that her salary allowed her to live alone. Tonight she badly needed peace and privacy to come to terms with the upheaval of the day.

Her flat was the top half of a modest semi on the outskirts of the town. She shared the garage, but a private outside stair at the back of the house led to a small balcony which ran the length of her sitting-room and tiny kitchen, with a view of long, narrow lawn bordered by a tangle of shrubbery.

Wearily Ellis stripped off her festive red suit and silk shirt and stood under a shower as cold as she could bear before getting into denims and T-shirt. What, she thought morosely, should she say to Matthew Canning tomorrow? In one short day she'd run the entire gamut of emotions from elation to despair. Her mind still reeled from the experience. But one thing was very certain. From now on, she knew beyond all doubt, life would be very different.

She would survive, of course. Ellis prided herself on her common sense. She'd suffered one or two dents to her heart during her twenty-eight years of existence, other than Charles, and knew from experience that life went on just the same. But, she thought with a sigh, she would miss him badly. Charles Longman had been an integral part of her life now for a long time.

Which, she admitted reluctantly at last, made his indifference in one area very wounding. He seemed oblivious of the fact that his departure left her without a job. Did he feel nothing at all for her? Today, when he'd kissed her for the first time, she'd been so sure that he saw her clearly at last, as a flesh and blood woman with feelings. Not that she'd have allowed the kiss to go on, of course, even if Matthew Canning hadn't interrupted. She would have passed the incident off lightly as a farewell gesture, a mere token of affection after their years together. Besides, a kiss wasn't what she'd wanted. Some concern about her future would have been far more welcome. Charles didn't seem to care two hoots about it, other than to think she'd apply for the job with the new managing director, as everyone seemed to expect.

Ellis scowled into the distance. Everyone was right, of course. She'd be a fool not to work for Matthew Canning—at least until she found another job, and a job in Pennington at that, now she'd bought her own flat, or at least somewhere within a radius of a few miles. Driving, to Ellis, was very much a chore, and her car purely a means of getting to work or visiting her mother at weekends.

Next morning, slightly less depressed after sleeping far better than expected, Ellis arrived in the car park to find Matthew Canning's Lotus there before her. She eyed it with hostility, her day spoiled before it had even begun. This morning there was no dawdle on her way to her office. Today was a day to be got through as best she could, with no time for gazing at views which, in any case, were obscured today by rain, in keeping with her mood.

Ellis rarely wore black, which tended to quench her natural colour. To match her funereal mood she wore a tailored navy suit with a severe, collarless jacket and slim skirt, with only a crisp white lawn handkerchief tucked into one of the breast pockets to soften the effect. Knowing it would be an hour at least before Charles Longman put in an appearance, Ellis checked all was well with his office, then immersed herself in a maze of facts and figures to pass on to Alison Blake, the development surveyor of Spa Properties.

'You start early,' said Matthew Canning from the doorway a few minutes later. He smiled slightly. 'Good morning. I did knock. You were too busy to hear.'

'Good morning. Can I do anything for you, Mr Canning?' Surely he didn't want an answer straight away! Ellis pushed her glasses up her nose as she looked at him in query.

'I merely wondered what time Longman gets in.'

'About nine, usually.'

'Every day?'

Ellis nodded, ignoring the occasions when Charles Longman arrived much later than that.

Matthew Canning surprised her by perching himself on the corner of her desk. He looked alert and very fit, a slight, healthy colour in his tanned, close-shaven cheeks, his eyes clear, his tawny hair glossy, his shirt pristinely white above a dark suit cut with a skill to match any of Charles Longman's. 'And you, Miss Worth? Are you always in at this time?'

'Always, Mr Canning, except for the rare occasions when I'm ill.'

Matthew Canning stood up. 'Highly commendable. What time can I expect the rest of the workforce?'

Ellis informed him that most employees arrived by eight-thirty.

'I see.' He strolled to the door. 'When Longman finally deigns to put in an appearance, give me a ring, will you? I'd like to talk to you both straight away before I see Hennessy.'

'Very well, Mr Canning.'

'Good. I'll expect you later.' He turned, brows raised slightly above the chill grey gaze. 'But not too *much* later, please.'

Ellis glared at the quietly closed door with hostility. Oh, please, she prayed fervently, please let Charles take it into his head to arrive before nine for once. Her prayers went unanswered. Charles was even later than usual. It was nine-thirty by the time he put in an appearance, and almost ten before he'd allow her to ring the managing director's office.

'Have a heart,' he shuddered, washing aspirin down with coffee. 'Let me get myself together a bit before I cope with Genghis Khan.'

Ellis was not amused. It was blatantly obvious that Charles was suffering from a blinding hangover, and for once she was completely out of sympathy with him. The reason for it was obvious enough. She knew, better than anyone, what a crushing blow he'd suffered. Nevertheless she had fully expected him to get in on time today, of all days.

While Charles was pulling himself together Ellis assembled the various lists of information she'd stayed late to compile the night before in readiness for the encounter with the new managing director.

'I thought you might like to run your eyes over these,' she said bracingly. 'In case Mr Canning requires facts and figures.'

Charles took them without enthusiasm, eyeing the neat, detailed précis with a yawn. 'Thanks, Ellis.' He gave her rather a sheepish smile. 'By the way, ring the usual florist before we get started—send some red roses to Monica Caldwell, The Priory, Little Reeve, would you?'

'What message?'

He scowled. 'Don't look so po-faced, Ellis. It was all perfectly innocent. Clissy was off eventing as usual with her beloved gee-gees, so I called in on Monica on my way home for tea and sympathy and she let me cry on her shoulder, that's all.'

'I see. What message would you like on the card for Mrs Caldwell?' repeated Ellis stonily.

'Just say "Thanks for cheering me up. Love, Charlie."'

Charlie!

Ellis returned to her office, rigid with distaste, rang the florist as she had so many times in the past on similar errands, then, with some reluctance, rang the managing director's office. 'Ellis Worth, Mr Canning. Is it a convenient time for the meeting right now, please?'

'It's been convenient any time this past hour,' he snapped.

'Mr Longman apologises. He was delayed.'

'Was he indeed? Tell him I expect you both in ten minutes. Having waited this long, I'll damn well finish my coffee in peace first.'

Ellis put down the phone, utterly depressed at the prospect of playing pig in the middle between Charles and the new managing director.

'Mr Canning wants to see us in ten minutes,' she announced, going into the other office.

Charles grimaced. 'Like going up before the Beak.' He stared at Ellis, seeing her clearly, it was obvious, for the first time that day. 'I say, you don't look your usual blooming self, Ellis. Not ill, are you?'

No! Ellis wanted to scream. I'm not ill, I'm just worried and upset and if you didn't have such a hangover perhaps you'd understand why.

'I'm fine,' she said woodenly.

'Good girl.' He sighed. 'What the blazes will I do without you?'

'There'll be someone else at CCS.'

'Ah, but will she understand me as well as you do?'

Probably not, thought Ellis as she glanced at her watch. 'Right. Time we were on our way. Mr Canning's been waiting to see you since the crack of dawn.'

Charles shrugged indifferently. 'Too bad. Can't see what the devil he wants with me anyway.'

He was soon to find out. Once the three of them were in Mr Maitland's room, Charles and Ellis seated in front of the large mahogany desk, Matthew Canning at ease in the swivel chair behind it, the latter went straight to the point, demanding facts and figures relevant to everything accomplished in the sales sector under Charles Longman's brief directorial aegis at Colcraft Holdings.

Time and time again Charles Longman paused in his discourse to turn to Ellis, and each time she swiftly supplied the necessary information, her voice unobtrusive as she filled in the gaps. Matthew Canning fired questions at a rate which plainly worsened the pain in Charles Longman's head until the latter could barely think. At the end of one of the most uncomfortable hours Ellis had spent in her entire life the new managing director rose to his feet, a bland smile on his face as he thanked them both.

'I'm grateful to both of you for your time,' he said smoothly. 'It's been most illuminating.'

Charles Longman muttered something unintelligible, turned a ghastly colour, and fled.

'Mr Longman has a migraine,' Ellis said stiffly.

Matthew Canning grinned, looking suddenly human. 'Pull the other one, Miss Worth; I know a hangover when I see it. I don't blame him. In his particular situation I'd have tied one on myself last night.'

Ellis made no comment as she packed papers into folders.

'Now, Miss Worth, have you made any decision about the job we discussed last night?' he asked briskly.

Ellis picked up the folders, then looked at him levelly. 'May I be frank, Mr Canning?'

'Of course.'

'If I followed my instincts I'd leave at the end of the week.'

The light eyes hardened. 'No taste for life after Longman, I assume.'

'That has nothing to do with it!' she snapped. 'If you must know, Mr Canning, I'm human enough to feel hurt. After nine years' service with Colcraft it appears that no one, apart from the other secretarial staff, seems the least bit concerned about *my* fate.'

'You're wrong,' he said flatly. 'Oliver Maitland was, for one. He insisted you were the ideal person to work for me, if it makes you feel better.'

It made Ellis feel a lot better. 'How very kind of Mr Maitland.'

'But since we're dealing in truth here, Miss Worth, I'd better make it clear I have my doubts.' He flung out a hand as she stiffened. 'No. Hear me out. It's no secret that your loyalties lie with Longman, which, miracle of efficiency though you may be, I regard as a major disadvantage. On the other hand I admit I need someone right away, which is why I suggested you come to me on a temporary basis.'

'I see,' she said, with a sudden longing to tell him exactly what he could do with his temporary job.

'Good.' He paused, studying her hostile face. 'But let's use the word "trial" instead of temporary—make it a trial period of three months. If, at the end of that time, or, indeed, any time beforehand, you *or* I think the arrangement won't work, it can be terminated— with due notice on either side, of course.'

Ellis digested this in silence for a moment. 'I'd like a few more hours' grace to decide, Mr Canning.'

He smiled briefly. 'Very well, Miss Worth. I'm a reasonable man. Let me know by tonight.'

Ellis returned to her office like a fugitive seeking sanctuary. She slumped in the chair behind her desk, then swivelled it round so that she could look through the window at the rooftops of Pennington Spa.

What a start to the day! Charles had come off really badly during the interview with the dynamic Mr Canning. She had known he would, of course, even without the drawback of the hangover. It had been like pitting a sleek stag against a man-eating tiger.

She sighed. Fond though she was of him, Ellis saw Charles Longman in a very clear light. She might be in love with him, in a cerebral, hero-worshipping kind of way, but she knew perfectly well he looked on her in return rather in the light of a guardian angel always on hand to listen to his problems and, nine times out of ten, to provide a solution for them. Charles made no secret of the fact that his wife was unsympathetic, that she took no interest in his problems whatsoever. With no children to take up her time, Clarissa Longman sublimated her maternal yearnings in her beloved horses, oblivious to the fact that her husband sought discreet consolation elsewhere. Only Ellis, who sent the flowers and bought the occasional tasteful gift, knew the facts.

But I'm going to miss him badly just the same, she thought sadly. For years she'd seen him almost every working day, from the time she'd left the typing pool to become his secretary. Charles Longman had been different in those days, eager and work-hungry, not satisfied until he'd reached the dizzy heights of directorship. But after Ellis became an Associate of the Institute of Chartered Secretaries and Administrators, things began to change gradually. Charles had been oddly smug when she qualified, in a Pygmalion sort of way, as though he alone were responsible for her success, and from then on began to lean on her more and more, to the extent that sometimes she wondered if he realised how much.

'Ellis!'

She leapt to her feet in response to the familiar parade-ground tones of Oliver Maitland. 'Mr Maitland, I'm sorry, I didn't hear you.'

'Shouldn't you be at lunch, my dear, instead of daydreaming in here on your own?' His shrewd old eyes bored into hers. 'Bit upset, are you?'

'Yes,' admitted Ellis, too depressed to dissemble.

'News about Charles came as a bit of a shock, no doubt.' He wagged an admonitory finger at her.

'Needn't affect you, Ellis. Young Canning's a good man. You'll enjoy working for him.'

Ellis looked doubtful. 'I'm not sure yet I intend to work for him, Mr Maitland.'

'I hope you're not dithering due to some quixotic loyalty to Charles!' He smiled kindly. 'Take my advice and work for Canning. I told him myself he'd be damn lucky to get a secretary like you, my dear.'

Ellis felt very touched. During her time at Colcraft she'd had very little to do with Oliver Maitland in person. 'That's very kind of you,' she said gratefully. 'Thank you.'

'No more than the truth, Ellis.' He consulted the watch hanging from a gold chain strung across his waistcoat. 'Must get on. Lot to do before I go out to pasture.' He shot an imperious look at her. 'By the way, I expect you to come to this do I'm giving tonight. Eight sharp in the boardroom, drinks and a buffet supper. No excuses. Muriel said I was to make sure you didn't wriggle out of it.'

Ellis smiled. She liked Mrs Maitland, a lady well known in Pennington for her tireless work for charity. 'How kind of her. Thank you. Tell her I'll be there.'

The rest of the day was chaotically busy. The meeting in the morning had made such a hole in the time allotted for a report needed urgently next day that Ellis only noticed Charles was missing for most of the afternoon when he put his head round her door at one stage to apologise for his absence.

'Anything I need to know?' he asked, still looking rather green around the gills. 'Report ready yet?'

'There's a pile of mail on your desk waiting to be signed, but I won't have the draft of this report for you to look over until tomorrow,' she informed him, in no mood for apology. 'And Mr Maitland sent a message via his secretary to remind you that you're expected at his farewell party this evening.' Ellis met Charles's bloodshot eyes significantly. 'I said you'd be delighted, Mr Longman.'

Charles groaned like a man in pain, said something brief and vulgar about the party, then bolted back into his office. Ten minutes later he was gone for the day, before Ellis had a chance to say she'd see him later. Not, she thought wearily as she got in the car, that she was in any mood for a party. But a personal invitation from the Maitlands was tantamount to a royal command.

By the time she got home, Ellis, who had skipped lunch, was starving. She disposed of a hearty sandwich while she ran a bath, allowed herself a few minutes for an unwinding wallow in hot water, then shampooed her hair, blessing its clever cut which needed only a few minutes to blow dry into perfect shape. Afterwards she took great care in choosing something to wear, needing the assurance of knowing she looked her best. Clarissa Longman, when she troubled to get out of jodhpurs, was a very elegant lady.

Ellis eventually settled for a ribbed silk skirt in her favourite bitter chocolate shade, and an unlined oyster silk jackct. As she added heavy gilt earrings and a gilt bracelet of manacle proportions, she wondered what the new MD's wife was like. Matthew Canning himself was so sure and confident and all of a piece that it was hard to imagine him against a background of domesticity, with children and toys cluttered about him.

Ten minutes later Ellis was back in her place in the Colcraft car park, feeling as though she'd never left it. Why, she thought bitterly, had she ever said she'd come? Her gloom deepened as she emerged from the lift into a wave of noise and laughter coming from the boardroom.

'Ellis, good to see you!' called Oliver Maitland from the open doorway. 'Muriel was wondering where you were. Let me give you some champagne.'

'How delightful you look, my dear,' said Mrs Maitland, who was wearing a blue silk dress which could have gone anywhere from a church council meeting to a formal dinner, and probably did. 'You know all the men, of course, but are there any ladies you haven't met?'

'I don't think so.' Ellis accepted the champagne with thanks.

'Then off you go and circulate, my dear.'

Given a warm reception by a crowd of younger management people from sales, Ellis was soon laughing and chatting, enjoying herself despite the expected fusillade of questions about the new changes at the top in Colcraft. After a while some of the wives protested about so much shop talk, demanding a change to more general topics, at which point Ellis noticed that the Longmans had arrived.

Ellis felt the usual pang of enmity as she saw Clarissa Longman. Anything less like the depressed wife of a demoted husband was hard to imagine. Clarissa wore her heavy blonde hair straight and shoulder-length, in a pale, silken frame for her tanned face, in sensational contrast to the bright jade of her silk suit. She gleamed like a jewel alongside the dark good looks of her husband, who, Ellis realised with a sinking heart, had started drinking long before his arrival.

'Clissy Longman's a stunner, isn't she?' said one of the men, to a concerted murmur of assent from both sexes. 'She doesn't seem bothered by the move.'

Ellis had no intention of discussing the Longmans. She excused herself swiftly and went off to talk to the company secretary, who was an elderly bachelor with a hearty dislike of gatherings of this nature.

'Hello, Mr Baker. How are you?'

'All the better for seeing you, Ellis, my dear.' He smiled at her with unconcealed pleasure, plainly glad of the chance to discuss the new changes in management. 'Canning's a high flyer,' he said at one stage. 'I fancy he'll effect quite a transformation at Colcraft. Not that it'll affect me much. I'll be retiring next year.'

'So soon? Why retire so young?' demanded Ellis with such patent sincerity that Godfrey Baker smiled, gratified.

'Flatterer! Next year will see the end of thirty years' service in one capacity or another with Colcraft. They've had their pound of flesh, Ellis. I've got a cottage in Cornwall, ready and waiting for the day I retire. I shall spend my time fishing and listening to tall stories from the men who do it for a living.'

'Good for you!'

'If you're not careful you'll end up working for Colcraft just as long, young lady. Brenda and I were talking about you today. She says it must be eight years or so since you first arrived on the scene.'

Ellis's smile was wry. 'I'm afraid I won't be around much longer, Mr Baker. The way things are right now there doesn't seem to be a permanent place for me. Where is Brenda tonight, by the way? Your invaluable right hand usually keeps you company at these things.'

'Not too well these days, our Brenda. All these years slaving away for me seem to have worn her down, poor woman. I asked her to come, but she pleaded a previous engagement with a novel and an early night.' Godfrey Baker's eyes lit with a shrewd gleam. 'And don't try to change the subject. Surely you're not leaving because of Longman, like some arcane Indian widow committing suttee on her husband's funeral pile, Ellis?'

She made a face. 'Gruesome idea! The truth is, Mr Baker, I think it's time I made a move. As you said, I've been at Colcraft a long time.'

Her companion gestured towards the door. 'Ah. Talking of our new leader—he's arrived. Praise be. Now we can eat.'

Ellis turned quickly, curious to see how Matthew Canning's wife would shape up to Clarissa Longman, but the tall, tawny-haired figure chatting to the Maitlands was unaccompanied.

'No Mrs Canning?' said Ellis in an undertone.

'No. He's a crusty bachelor like me!'

Ellis laughed, then looked doubtful as her companion annexed two more glasses of champagne from a passing waiter. 'I shouldn't, Mr Baker; I'm driving.'

'Take a taxi!' he advised, then looked across at the group in the doorway, which now included the Longmans. 'I see Clarissa's renewing her acquaintance with young Canning. They were in college together, you know.'

'No, I didn't.' Ellis had never associated college with Clarissa, who looked more like the product of an expensive finishing-school. The blonde, elegant Clarissa was obviously very much at home with Matthew Canning, Ellis noted, then tensed as she saw Charles

Longman leave his wife with his successor to make his way across the room towards her.

'How are you, Charles?' enquired Godfrey affably. 'Bearing up under the strain?'

'Just about,' said Charles, eyeing Ellis moodily. 'You look very smart tonight.'

'Thank you. Is your headache better?'

'It will be once I've had a drink.' He beckoned to a waiter and seized a glass of champagne, gulping it down like water.

Ellis met Godfrey's eyes as Charles called the waiter back for another, feeling rather like a mother wanting to make excuses for her child's behaviour. As Godfrey talked to Charles about the new move, Ellis realised she was being watched, and glanced up to find Clarissa Longman and Matthew Canning eyeing her in a way which made it clear that she was the object of their conversation. To Ellis's consternation Matthew Canning promptly brought Clarissa across the room to join them, the smile he gave Ellis putting her very much on her guard.

'How very beautiful you look, Clarissa,' said Godfrey smoothly. 'May I get you a drink?'

'Thank you, Godfrey, but I've already had my quota. I'm chauffeur tonight—as usual.' Clarissa directed a hostile look in her husband's direction before turning to Ellis with a glittering smile. 'Long time no see, Ellis.'

'Good evening, Mrs Longman——'

'Oh, Clarissa, please. Even Clissy, if you like.' The smile widened. 'It isn't as though Charles is your boss any more.'

'Too true,' said Charles sulkily. 'This may be a celebration for Maitland and Canning, but from my
point of view it's more of a bloody wake.'

'Nonsense, Charles,' said his wife maliciously.
'You'll adore being a big fish in a little pond. Right
up your street. Though how you'll manage without
your wonderful Ellis I can't imagine.'

Ouch, thought Ellis. She looked about her for a
means of escape, and found it in the last quarter she'd
have expected as Matthew Canning exchanged a look
with Clarissa, then smiled blandly at the others.

'Forgive me if I steal Miss Worth away to talk shop
for a while. Have you heard she's going to exchange
one slave-driver for another next week by coming to
work for me?'

Godfrey Baker stepped into the awkward little
hiatus hastily, congratulating Matthew Canning on
his good fortune, while Clarissa murmured something saccharine with a cat-like little smile. Charles
stared in bitter accusation at Ellis, as if she'd committed some heinous crime. Which, in Charles
Longman's eyes, she probably had, she thought in
anguish as she found herself hustled off to the buffet
table, where Matthew Canning deftly filled two plates
with assorted delicacies and took her to sit a discreet
distance from the nearest group of people.

Ellis speared a prawn viciously and chewed on it
for a moment before she could trust herself to speak.
'Was that necessary, Mr Canning? Nothing was settled
regarding this trial run you spoke about, if you
remember.'

'My dear Miss Worth, I merely hurried things up
a bit. If you'd meant to refuse you'd have done so

before now.' His eyes met her quizzically. 'Am I right?'

Ellis wanted badly to say no, but deep down she knew he was right. The temporary job was the only sensible course to take. And not even her worst enemy could accuse her of being anything but sensible, she thought bitterly. Except where Charles was concerned, and that, thank heaven, was a weakness known to no one but herself. 'Yes,' she said at last. 'Which is just as well, since now you've made a public announcement about it I don't have much choice in the matter anyway.'

'That had occurred to me,' he admitted smoothly, disposing of his meal with a relish Ellis envied. 'Frankly it seemed the ideal way to kill two birds with one stone.'

'In what way?'

'I relieved you of making a decision you obviously see as a disloyalty to Longman. It also gave me an excuse to get you away from Clarissa.'

Ellis choked a little on a mouthful of chicken. It was a moment or two later before she could ask him what he meant.

Matthew Canning looked down at her with an odd expression in his eyes. 'I used to know Clarissa quite well at one time, but I've rather lost touch since her marriage to Longman. She's changed quite a lot—seems to need to hit out at the world these days. It seemed best to remove you from the line of fire.'

'Why should Mrs Longman feel the need to hit out at me?' asked Ellis coldly, losing all enthusiasm for the food left on her plate.

One sepia brow rose slightly. 'Why, indeed?'

She frowned. 'What do you mean?'

He looked scornful. 'Don't be naïve. I'm referring to the touching little scene I interrupted yesterday.'

Ellis flushed. 'That, Mr Canning, was by nature of goodbye. Mr Longman and I have worked together for several years. Surely one solitary moment of sentiment was allowable after all that time?'

'My dear Miss Worth,' he said, taking her plate, 'it's nothing to do with me. It's Clarissa you should be convincing. Be warned. She suspects you harbour rather warmer feelings for her husband than you should. She was about to have fun at your expense, I fancy, so I diverted her by leaking the news which would have been common knowledge tomorrow anyway.'

'You needn't have troubled yourself, Mr Canning,' Ellis said tartly. 'There's nothing at all between myself and Mr Longman.'

'I didn't say there was. I'd lay odds he doesn't have a clue how you feel—his perception isn't sufficient for him to cotton on, Miss Worth.'

Ellis eyed him with hostility, then dropped her eyes hastily before anyone noticed.

'I'll tell you why you're angry, too,' he offered calmly.

'I know perfectly well why I'm angry!'

'It's nothing to do with the fact that I guessed your little secret. You're angry with me for saying Charles doesn't have the sense to realise it.' Matthew Canning smiled at her with an air of self-congratulation which made Ellis itch to throw something at him.

But after a moment or two of fraught silence her clear-thinking brain acknowledged, grudgingly, the truth of his statement.

'You're like a mother hen where he's concerned,' he went on. 'This morning you were in like lightning the moment he began to run down, ready with your facts and figures like a pet computer on a lead.' His lips curved in a social, polite smile at startling odds with the sardonic expression in the light, bright eyes locked with hers.

Suddenly Ellis was struck by the enormity of his observation. She had been so sure that her feelings for Charles were a secret no one knew. But if this man had homed in on it after meeting her only once or twice perhaps everyone else at Colcraft was in on it too. She darted a look about the room, but no one seemed in the least concerned with them. There was a rather motherly, approving smile from Mrs Maitland, and a black look from Charles, but otherwise the noisy occupants of the boardroom seemed far too intent on enjoying themselves to care what Matthew Canning was discussing with Charles Longman's secretary.

'Don't worry,' he said. 'It doesn't show.'

'If you could tell straight away, it must,' she said, distraught.

Matthew Canning took her plate. 'Stay there. I'll get you some dessert.'

Ellis gagged at the mere thought. After what he'd just told her it seemed unlikely she'd ever want to eat again. 'Not for me, thank you.'

He shrugged, then went back to the table, laughing and chatting with several people en route before he returned to Ellis with an iced soufflé in one hand and a man-sized plate of cheese and biscuits in the other.

'I hope you like this sort of thing.'

Ellis eyed her offering with dislike. 'I said I didn't want anything—thank you,' she added belatedly.

'Then just fiddle about with the spoon and pretend you're eating it. Give you something to do,' he advised.

Ellis did as he said. She even ate a spoonful of the soufflé, and found it so delicious that she managed one or two more before giving up. But in the end she couldn't keep back the question burning in her brain.

'Are my feelings written all over my face then, Mr Canning?'

Matthew Canning gave her a considering look. 'No. Quite the reverse. Despite the kiss, if I hadn't seen you both together this morning I'd never have guessed. But during our meeting you were so desperate to cover up for Longman, jumping in every time he floundered. Not,' he added, 'that the vibes you gave out were in the least sexual. To be brutally honest you were more like a mother trying to cover up for her child.'

Ellis traced patterns in her soufflé with the tip of her spoon. 'How amusing all this must be for you.' She gave him a twisted little smile. 'You know, Mr Canning, this conversation wouldn't be taking place if I were staying on at Colcraft. I'd as soon come to work in my nightgown as say anything remotely personal to Mr Maitland.'

'I'm aware of that,' he assured her with irony. 'And it might make you feel better to know that Oliver Maitland isn't the only one who thinks it would be a crying shame for Colcraft to lose a bright, intelligent lady like you, Miss Worth.'

Ellis, still horrified by the fact that her secret was no longer her own, wasn't to be diverted. 'It doesn't seem to matter any more. Under the circumstances, I think the sooner I leave Colcraft the better.'

Suddenly someone banged on the table. There were appeals for silence as Oliver Maitland made a witty speech, rounding it off by thanking all present for the handsome silver tea service presented as a parting gift. As soon as the applause died down Ellis smiled politely at Matthew Canning.

'I must go. Thank you for—for your company. Goodnight.'

He inclined his head impersonally. 'Goodnight.'

Desperate to get away, Ellis had to force herself to chat with various people on her way to the door. At last she was able to wish the Maitlands a happy retirement, managing to avoid contact with both Longmans, then escape from the room with a soaring sense of relief. Alone in the lift, she slumped against a wall, eyes closed, then hurried out into the car park into the twilight, almost breaking into a run as she got to her car. When she reached it she could have wept like a baby. One of the tyres had a puncture. And Ellis knew as much about changing tyres as piloting a spacecraft to the moon. She aimed an angry kick at the offending wheel, then hurried from the car park at top speed before anyone could see her. It was a good half-hour's walk to her flat in Sycamore Road, but since there was no alternative Ellis set out at a punishing pace, cursing shoes better suited to carpets than pavements. To make her misery complete she'd gone only a short way before the unmistakable black Lotus cruised to a stop beside her.

'Can I give you a lift?' asked Matthew Canning.

Ellis gave up. All she wanted in the world was to go home to bed. And if he gave her a lift she'd get there all the faster.

'Yes,' she said baldly.

He leapt out to open the passenger door for her. 'Get in.'

Ellis obeyed, but eyed him sternly as he started up the car. 'Don't drive too fast, please; I get car-sick.'

His mouth tightened. 'I keep to speed-limits religiously, I swear, Miss Worth. Where do you live?'

Ellis supplied the address, then took refuge in silence as the car glided smoothly through the brightly lit town centre.

'You probably won't want my advice,' he observed after a time, 'but I wouldn't recommend walking home alone at night very often, if ever.'

'I don't.' She explained about the flat tyre.

'Why the hell didn't you come back inside and ring for a taxi?'

'I couldn't face going back in there.' Suddenly she was fiercely glad her time with Colcraft was coming to an end. The fact that the man beside her was Matthew Canning, the new managing director, didn't matter a damn any more. She could say what she liked and to blazes with him. 'Since you're the percipient one when it comes to people's feelings,' she said acidly, 'it won't come as a surprise to learn that at this moment in time all I want is to get home to bed, away from you, from Clarissa, from Charles Longman and the whole Colcraft shebang. Suddenly, Mr Canning, I've had it up to here with the entire organisation.'

He shot her a startled sidelong glance, then shook with sudden laughter. 'Good for you. Stand up for yourself. You've had a rough couple of days—do you good to blow your top. I won't say a word, I promise—about this, or our conversation earlier. But believe me, I'm not all that sensitive to people's feelings as a rule.' He gave a short laugh. 'Otherwise, my dear Miss Worth, I wouldn't be nearly so good at what I do. I can hire and fire with the best of them and never turn a hair. Yours is the only wavelength I've tuned in on in a very long time.'

Ellis shuddered. 'Then it's a good thing I'm leaving the company.

'What about Longman?'

'What about him?'

'Is your wavelength closed to him, too?'

Ellis gave an inelegant sniff. 'As you said earlier, Mr Canning, he has no idea how I feel about him. Wavelengths are not a speciality of his.'

'Do I detect a note of disenchantment?'

Ellis eyed him dispassionately as he brought the car to a halt outside her gate. 'I was wrong. You don't really understand at all. What I feel for Charles Longman is for the man as he is. With all faults. I see him very clearly—with my eyes wide open. I may wear spectacles in the office, but they're not rose-tinted, I assure you.'

Matthew Canning turned in his seat to look at her closely. 'I didn't imagine they were. But you're a hell of a sight more than just a secretary to Longman. To me—and not only to me—you're more like an alter ego, one who does more than a fair share of the work accredited to him.'

Ellis sat very still, digesting this. The man wasn't so far wrong, of course. Several of her ideas had been passed off by Charles as his own over the last year or two. She'd been so dazzled and flattered that she'd been only too pleased, of course; the perfect secretary in every way.

'I must go,' she said quickly, fiddling with the seatbelt. 'Thank you so much for bringing me home——'

He pressed the catch to release her. 'You're angry again.'

'No. It just occurred to me I've been guilty of gross indiscretion.' Ellis scrambled hastily from her seat, intent on getting away quickly, but he was out of the car before her, by her side as she reached the gate.

'Everyone's human, Miss Worth,' he said flatly. 'But a word of advice. In future try to direct your loyalty into channels more worthy of them. You're too bright to go languishing after a married man. Particularly one who's married to Clarissa Longman.'

Ellis managed to hang on to her temper by reminding herself forcibly that she was committed to work for this man for the time being, which ruled out letting fly with her fist. 'Thank you for the lift, Mr Canning, but not for the advice. Goodnight.'

'Goodnight.' He raised a hand in salute, ducked back into the car and drove off.

CHAPTER THREE

ELLIS had hoped against hope to avoid Matthew Canning next day. Fate decreed otherwise. She ran into him in the foyer first thing the following morning and had no choice but to accompany him to the top floor in the lift. He commented pleasantly on the weather and the view, then took his leave with a brief, impersonal smile. Ellis felt light-headed with relief as she closed her office door behind her. The new MD quite plainly had no intention of indulging in further personal remarks. Now all she had to do was keep her head down, work hard for the short time necessary as his secretary, after which she could forget Colcraft and Matthew Canning, even Charles Longman in time, and get on with the rest of her life.

'So this is goodbye, Ellis,' said Charles Longman, late on Friday. He gave her a mournful grin. 'All this is so sudden that I keep feeling I'll wake up any minute and find it's a bad dream.'

'Far better to make a quick, clean break,' said Ellis, deliberately cheerful to hide her secret pain.

'I wish you were going with me to CCS.'

She shook her head, smiling faintly. 'You won't need me.'

Charles took her hand and squeezed it. 'I'm going to miss you like hell, Ellis.'

She knew how he felt. Life would be flat without the charm of Charles Longman to sweeten her working day. 'I'll miss you, too,' she said huskily, withdrawing her hand. 'Goodbye, Mr Longman. Good luck.'

He hesitated, eyed her uncertainly, then bent to kiss her cheek. 'Goodbye, Ellis. Good luck to you, too— even if you did desert me for the enemy.'

As he straightened the phone rang on her desk. Ellis picked it up, her throat constricting as for the last time she said 'Mr Longman's office.'

She listened for a moment, answered politely, then turned to Charles Longman, her face carefully blank. 'Monica Caldwell for you.'

He gave her a rueful grin, already on the way to his own office. 'Put her through, Ellis. Cheers.' He raised his hand in airy salute then shut his door.

It was not the way Ellis would have chosen to part with Charles Longman. With a sigh she put the call through, cast an eye over her orderly desk, then closed the door behind her as she left, feeling as if a chapter in her life had closed. Which was illogical, she knew quite well. It might be as long as three months before she could actually say that. None the less, today felt like the end of a chapter.

'You look shattered, darling,' said Polly Worth later that evening.

'I am, I am,' said Ellis as she climbed out of the car. 'Hello, love.' She put an arm around her mother and gave her a kiss, then turned to greet her aunt.

'Come and tell us all about it,' said Lydia Worth, taking her niece's bag. 'Let's have a drink on the lawn. Supper can hang about until you've relaxed a while.'

Once sprawled in a rickety old deckchair in the garden behind Briar Cottage, Ellis regaled her fascinated audience with an edited version of the week's happenings.

Polly shrugged philosophically. 'Can't say I'm sorry in one way.'

'No,' agreed Lydia. 'High time you broke loose from Charles Longman and lived your own life, my girl.'

'Amen to that,' agreed Polly. 'But Ellis has been hankering after that man for so long that she's bound to be like a lost soul for a bit.'

Ellis gazed at her parent aghast. 'You knew?'

'Of course, child. It worried us both—but we couldn't interfere.'

Ellis rolled her eyes heavenwards. 'I fondly thought I'd been nurturing my secret deep in my bosom for years unknown to a soul, yet this is the second time this week it's been mentioned. Am I so utterly transparent, for heaven's sake?'

'Oh, *I* wouldn't have known,' Lydia assured her. 'Your mother told me.'

'How did *you* know?' demanded Ellis, turning on her mother.

'I didn't, exactly. I just had my suspicions.' Polly smiled apologetically. 'At one time, you see, you were always out with some young man or other, even before Michael. But after you broke off your engagement and started studying for your ACIS you never seemed to have time for fun any more. All you talked about was your work. And Charles Longman. And when you talked about *him* there was a look in your eye which worried me to death.'

'It would have worried me, too,' said Ellis with feeling, 'if I'd known about it. And I thought I'd been so clever!' She gave a cracked little laugh. 'Well, my dears, you need worry no more. Charles has gone, and as soon as I can I'll be gone too, preferably to work in a place where the men are all single and available and falling over themselves to wine and dine little Ellis.'

'Are there any places like that?' enquired her aunt, laughing.

'I can dream, can't I?'

Later, over dinner, Polly Worth said curiously, 'Who was the other person, Ellis?'

'What other person?'

'Now then! You said someone else knew about your—your penchant for Charles Longman.'

Ellis pulled a face. 'Only the new managing director, no less—Mr Matthew Canning himself.'

The others looked so appalled that Ellis was quick to reassure them, telling them that in the circumstances it didn't matter a bit. After the end of Matthew Canning's stipulated trial period she need never see him again.

A weekend of cosseting was an effective, if temporary, morale booster. When Ellis drove back to Pennington on the Sunday evening, laden with home-baked delicacies and flowers from the garden of Briar Cottage, she felt more philosophical about life than she would have thought possible a day or two earlier.

She smiled fondly as she put her spoils away. It was five years now since her mother had sold the family home in Pennington. Mrs Worth had struggled to keep it up after her husband died, but eventually George Worth's sister Lydia, headmistress of a primary school most of her professional life, had suggested the three of them pool their resources and live together in the cottage bought for her retirement in a pretty Cotswold village within easy reach of Pennington Spa.

For a year or so the arrangement had worked well. But eventually Ellis had felt the urge to spread her wings a little. To begin with she'd shared a house with several other girls in the town, but a particularly generous salary increase one year had decided her to take the plunge and invest in her own flat in Sycamore Road. Now she felt she had the best of both worlds; a place of her own, plus a bolt-hole to run to whenever she needed it in the shape of Briar Cottage.

By the following morning Ellis's morale was on a downward curve again. The start of a new working week at Colcraft no longer filled her with anticipation. Everything would be so different from now on, a fact emphasised by the sight of the now familiar black car already in place in the slot marked 'Managing Director' when she arrived. As she entered the building she felt depressed, her former zest and anticipation conspicuous by its absence—vanished, it seemed, along with Charles Longman. Wondering how best to proceed, Ellis decided to take the bull by the horns and report to the managing director's office at once, early or not. Matthew Canning, as anticipated, was already hard at work at Oliver Maitland's desk.

At her knock he looked up with a cool smile. 'Good morning, Miss Worth. How was your weekend?'

'Good morning, Mr Canning. My weekend was very pleasant, thank you.'

'Good.' He waved her to the chair in front of the desk. 'Sit down, please. I won't be long.'

Ellis sat quietly, watching him as he finished making notes on the pile of papers in front of him. He looked very fit. His face wore the same early-morning flush of health she'd noted before. He positively exuded appetite for the new job. And in his own individual style he was just as elegant as Charles, too, she conceded grudgingly. The dark blue suit and creamy pink shirt looked good against his bright hair. His face was too sharply cut to be classically handsome like Charles's, of course, but quite attractive in a hawkish, emphatic sort of way. Pity his hair was red.

Losing interest, she turned her eyes to walls which showed oblongs of lighter paint where pictures had once hung. Oliver Maitland's leather·chesterfield and small Pembroke table were missing, too. Without them the room looked very bare.

'I shall redecorate,' said Matthew Canning, intercepting her look.

Ellis nodded. 'All the offices are due for a face-lift soon. I'd already helped Mr Longman choose the colour scheme for his.'

'Dan Hennessy will prefer to choose his own.'

'Yes, of course.' Ellis hesitated. 'Mr Canning, there are one or two things I need to clear up from last week. Shall I get on with them before I make a start with you?'

He nodded. 'But get your things moved to the office next door first, please.'

'Very well.'

'Have you come to terms with the thought of working for me yet, Miss Worth?' he asked bluntly.

'More or less, Mr Canning.' Her green eyes were non-committal as they met his. 'After all, it's only a temporary arrangement. Perhaps now is a good time to make it clear that at the end of it I intend to leave. It was never my intention to make Colcraft my life's work.'

'I see.' He stacked papers neatly in front of him, then leaned back in his chair, studying her. 'It may interest you to know the rest of management, even the board of directors, think you're the ideal person for this job.'

Ellis coloured slightly. 'That's very—very gratifying. I'm flattered.' She eyed him challengingly. 'Do you agree?'

'No.'

The negative hit her hard. It was one thing to decide against the job on a permanent basis, but another entirely to learn Matthew Canning didn't want her.

'I see,' she said stiffly, and half rose in her chair.

'Sit down, Miss Worth,' he ordered. 'Because you *don't* see. I merely meant that a woman of your qualifications should have her sights set on something higher, something more in line with her capabilities.'

Ellis subsided, eyeing him challengingly. 'I have. I'll utilise the time with you in looking round.'

'Very sensible.' He smiled. 'I hear along the grapevine that you make the best coffee in the building. Could we have some now?'

'Of course.'

Matthew Canning's eyebrows rose when Ellis returned with a tray set with the familiar Spode cups. 'Did Longman forget to take those with him?'

'No, Mr Canning.' She poured coffee with a steady hand. 'The cups are mine.'

He smiled. 'You know, Miss Worth, whatever you're being paid here can't possibly be enough.'

She shrugged as she sat down with her cup. 'My salary's perfectly adequate.'

'Are you aiming for a post which pays better?'

Ellis kept her eyes on her coffee. Now Charles Longman was no longer at Colcraft her main priority was to get away herself as quickly as possible. But as yet she'd had no stomach for the task of finding a new job, whether it paid well or not.

'I haven't really given it much thought yet,' she said truthfully at last, and looked up. 'At the risk of sounding conceited, Mr Canning, someone with my qualifications and experience shouldn't have too much trouble.'

'I'm damn sure you won't.' He held out his cup for more coffee. 'This is excellent, by the way.' He sipped appreciatively before going on. 'Now, I think you were offended by my note of discord in the general chorus of approval where you're concerned.'

Ellis shrugged. 'A little. I'm only human. But I quite understand that you prefer someone less—less set in different ways.'

Matthew Canning leaned forward in his seat slightly. 'If you mean ways you learnt with Charles Longman, you're right. I need a secretary, Miss Worth, not a nursemaid.'

Her eyes flashed. 'I resent that, Mr Canning. If you don't care for the way I fulfil my job you are, of course, at liberty to accept my notice as from today.'

'For crying out loud—don't be so damn touchy! What I meant,' he went on with exaggerated patience, 'is that working for me will be a different kettle of fish from your job with Longman. Unlike him, I don't actually need someone programmed to jog my memory and hand out advice, much less to deal with problems all by herself if necessary. I can do that all by *my*self. I simply need an intelligent woman familiar with all the necessary office technology, able to write good English and capable of diplomacy when necessary, particularly over the phone. Which is why, much as I value your services, I personally think you're wasted in this particular job.'

'I see.'

'But working for me will be no rest cure, believe me!' he warned her quickly.

Ellis did believe him. Even on such short acquaintance it was pretty obvious that Matthew Canning was a workaholic likely to give short shrift to anyone disinclined to pull his—or her—weight.

'By the way,' he said, making an obvious effort to put things on a friendlier footing, 'I was impressed to learn you're that favourite of clichés, the young temp who worked her way to the top.'

Ellis accepted the olive branch gingerly. 'Yes. I started my career by temping for one of the reputable agencies. I'd been working for them for just over a year when I was sent to Colcraft. At the end of my temping spell here I was offered a permanent place in the typing pool, and from there, eventually, I progressed to being Charles Longman's secretary.'

'It was a damn lucky day for him when you did.' He looked her in the eye. 'It seems to me that Longman's progress up the Colcraft ladder owes more to you than he's willing to admit.'

Ellis returned the look stonily, mentally hurling the olive branch on the floor, stamping on it.

'Well, Miss Worth? Shall we call a truce and try to rub along together as smoothly as possible?'

'You can be sure, Mr Canning, that any difficulties in our relationship won't come from me,' she said coldly.

His face hardened. 'Good. I never make promises I can't keep, so I can't guarantee there'll be no difficulties on my part. You'll find me a very different proposition from Longman, I'm afraid.'

'I've no doubt of that, Mr Canning. Is that all?'

'For now.' He returned to the work in front of him, looking up as she carried the tray to the door. 'See to your move first, then finish whatever it is you have to do. I'd like to make a start after lunch.'

'I'll be free before then, if you need me,' she offered.

'I won't. As I said, we'll start after lunch.' He was immersed in his work almost before he'd finished speaking.

Ellis seethed as she went through the connecting door to inspect the office which had once been the domain of the terrifying Miss Morrison. Yes, sir, no, sir, three bags full Mr Managing Director, she thought with venom.

During the time it took to stow her belongings away in her new office, Ellis became convinced the entire exercise was a waste of time. The more she thought about it the more convinced she became. She could never work in harmony with Matthew Canning. After lunch she'd tell him to stuff his job. He'd made it plain he considered her unsuitable for it anyway. As his secretary she'd have nothing to do except carry out his orders—working on her own initiative would soon be nothing but a fond memory of her time with Charles. A sudden pang of pain smote her. Besides, if she was completely honest with herself, she just didn't want to stay here now Charles was gone. She missed him badly, expected to see him every time she looked up from her desk or got out of a lift. She missed the cajoling smile and the drawling voice and his flattering dependence on her. She doubted if Matthew Canning had ever depended on anyone in his entire life.

Once Ellis was satisfied every last loose end from her former job was tied up ready for Vicky Fisher, she sat down in her new office to compose a very formal letter of resignation. Matthew Canning could hardly clap her in gaol if she left right away. As far as she was concerned the trial period was over. As soon as he returned from lunch she would present him with her resignation before he said a word.

Matthew Canning, she found, had several words to say, and none of them easy on the ear. After a quick look at the letter she flung down in front of him like a gauntlet, his eyes narrowed to crescents of ice. 'So you're reneging on your promise!'

'I wouldn't put it quite like that,' she said defensively, feeling like a prisoner in the dock as she stood in front of his desk.

'I would.' His eyes raked her flushed face. 'What made you change your mind?'

Ellis opted for truth. 'While I was moving my things I had time to think, Mr Canning.'

'Always a dangerous pastime for a woman!'

She eyed him with dislike, but kept silent. With an effort.

'Go on,' he encouraged, 'or shall I go on for you? Shall I tell you what *I* think changed your mind?'

Ellis threw caution to the winds. 'Please do. I'm sure you're going to anyway, Mr Canning, whether I want you to or not!'

'Sit down,' he snapped.

'I'd rather stand.'

'I *said* sit down!'

Ellis sat. She folded her hands in her lap, finger-nails biting into her palms.

Matthew Canning leaned back in his chair, his eyes cold in his set face. 'I think you just can't face the reality of life at Colcraft now Longman's no longer here, Miss Worth. In fact it wouldn't surprise me to hear you'd applied to CCS begging to work with him there.'

Ellis glared at him. 'That's outrageous!'

He shrugged. 'All right. I take back the part about running after him to CCS, but I'm damn certain about the other bit. Your first glimpse of what it would be like to work for me put you off completely, didn't it?'

'Certainly not. It wasn't the work which made me change my mind,' she assured him bitingly. 'It was the nature of it. I dislike the thought of never working on my own initiative, of never making a decision for myself. And,' she added, deciding to go the whole hog, 'it seemed to me that rubbing along together, as you put it, would not only be difficult, but downright impossible.' There, she thought triumphantly. Now you'll be glad to get rid of me.

He regarded her in silence for so long that Ellis was hard put to it not to fidget. 'To hark back to a recent conversation of ours, you don't understand me, either, Miss Worth. I never resist a challenge.' And, holding her eyes very deliberately, he tore up her resignation and threw the pieces in his waste-paper basket. 'I refuse to accept your resignation, Miss Worth.'

Ellis was speechless for a moment. 'But you can't make me work for you against my will!' she managed at last.

He shrugged. 'I can't manacle you to your desk, certainly. But I can withhold a reference. Since you've worked here at Colcraft for almost your entire professional career, it might be difficult to find another job without one.'

Ellis could hardly believe her ears. 'There are other people here at Colcraft, Mr Canning, any one of whom would be glad to give me a reference!'

'Not if I instructed them to do otherwise.'

There was dead silence in the room. Ellis stared down at her hands in rage, looking up at last to find Matthew Canning regarding her with cold complacence. She was saved from saying something regrettable by the intrusion of the phone. She rose automatically to answer it, listened for a moment, then said,

'I'll see if he's available.' She pressed a switch then raised an eyebrow at Matthew Canning. 'Jim Benson, Shire Textiles. Are you in?'

When he nodded she flicked the switch again and handed over the receiver, making her escape with relief.

Ellis collected her handbag from her office then went off to the cloakroom to wash her face and generally put herself back together after the gruelling little run-in with the new MD. What now? she asked her reflection. He's got you by the throat, Ellis Worth. Kick and scream all you like, but all you can do in the long run is buckle down and work for the wretched man. Because if you don't you haven't a hope in hell of working for someone else without a reference, qualified or not.

Hair and face restored to normal, Ellis went back into her office to be greeted by the buzzer demanding her presence. Taking her time, she put away her handbag, straightened her jacket then went through into the other office. 'Yes, Mr Canning?' she enquired. 'Are you ready to get on with your mail now?'

The cool grey eyes held a glint of admiration as he waved her to a chair. 'Yes, I'm ready. The point is, Miss Worth, are you? A few minutes ago you were ready to shake the dust of Colcraft from your shoes forever. Have I changed your mind?'

She shrugged, her emotions well under control by this time. 'Very effectively, Mr Canning. Without a reference I know perfectly well any hope of getting the type of job I want is pretty remote.'

'If you work for me the prescribed three-month period,' he said swiftly, 'I'll give you such a glowing reference that you'll have people falling over themselves to employ you. So, are we agreed?'

'Agreed,' she said without emotion. 'Three months, Mr Canning.' Which, she thought bitterly, as they tackled the work waiting for them, was likely to seem more like three years.

'I'm so relieved you're working for Mr Canning,' said Vicky Fisher at lunch next day. 'I felt positively criminal, putting you out of a job.'

'It wasn't your fault!'

Sarah Lewis, who worked in Personnel, eyed Ellis with envy. 'You are lucky,' she said wistfully. 'It must be wonderful to work for a man like Mr Canning.'

Ellis stared at her, astonished. 'Why?'

Vicky grinned. 'Pretty obvious, really. The rest of us work for staid married men, while you, ducky, spend your time closeted with Mr Dynamite, the most eligible bachelor in a twenty-mile radius.'

'And get paid for doing it!' added Sarah, chuckling.

And nothing Ellis could say would convince them that she was not only far from thrilled about her new job, but determined to leave it the moment the agreed three-month period was over.

Life moved up into another gear. Far from being any rest cure, working for Matthew Canning was a very demanding way to spend the day. From first thing in the morning until she left her office, invariably late, Ellis found herself fully extended as Matthew Canning settled into the new role which fitted him like a glove from the start. It was only a short time before Ellis found herself thinking of the old days with a longing which had nothing to do with Charles Longman. Her time as Charles's secretary seemed like some happy, leisured dream compared with the effort of keeping up with a human dynamo like Matthew Canning.

But, contrary to his forecast, it wasn't long before she was dealing with a great deal of routine affairs on her own after all. Sheer pressure of work, she thought with a secret malice, prevented the dynamic new broom from sweeping in quite every direction.

Ellis had soon learned the personal idiosyncrasies of an employer who strongly disliked formality. He preferred to be known as 'Matt' Canning, which was the way he answered the phone, and the name he ordered typed under his signature, without the title of managing director below it.

'The title's on the new stationery heading,' he said curtly. 'Why use it twice?'

Why indeed? thought Ellis. Everyone knew exactly who was running Colcraft Holdings these days, herself included.

'Enjoying your new job?' asked Godfrey Baker, on his way through her office one day.

Ellis smiled philosophically. 'It certainly keeps me busy! But it's only a temporary arrangement, until Mr Canning finds someone else.'

'Rubbish.' The shrewd eyes twinkled. 'Colcraft can't lose a clever girl like you. Tell him to give you a rise.'

'Come in, Godfrey,' said Matt from the doorway. 'Stop chatting up my secretary. She's got too much on her plate to waste time on old philanderers like you.'

Ellis listened to their laughter with resentment as Matt closed his office door. Too much on her plate was right, she thought, easing her aching back. Her new job entailed taking minutes at every meeting Matt Canning chaired, which at this initial stage took up an enormous amount of her working day. It was, she admitted, valuable experience. She learned a great deal as she listened to Matt Canning's plans for the rationalisation of Colcraft. His training at Harvard Business School was very much in evidence as he lectured forcefully on the vital practicalities of finance and marketing, on how to use power dynamics and specific methods to make the company organisationally effective. But transcribing his strictures into report form as quickly as he demanded was no mean task.

Ellis sighed as she glanced at her watch. She'd be even later getting home tonight than usual. But enough was enough. She committed the final paragraph of the report to her word processor's memory, then switched off her machine and tidied everything away. Matt Canning would just have to wait for the finished, printed article until Monday morning. Ellis

was halfway through her door when Matt called her
into his office over the intercom.

'Give me a hand before you go, Ellis,' he ordered
when she went in. He waved her to one end of the
desk. 'Help me shift this into the corridor, will you?
I rang down for some help, but I was too late. Everyone's gone.'

'It *is* almost seven,' said Ellis pointedly as she
stationed herself at one end of the huge new modern
desk Matt had bought to replace Oliver Maitland's.

'Sorry,' said Matt. 'Didn't notice the time. Shan't
keep you much longer. Now when I say heave, heave!'

Ellis eyed him with dislike. 'Do you mind if I take
my jacket off first? It's fairly new.'

'Hurry up then,' he said impatiently. 'The decorators are coming in a minute.'

'Tonight?' she panted as they manoeuvred the heavy
desk through the door. 'I thought they were coming
next weekend—ouch!' she wailed as her knuckles
grazed the door-handle.

'Didn't I say? I bullied them into coming a week
earlier—did you hurt yourself?' he asked, as they finally set the desk down in the corridor.

'Just a graze,' she snapped, sucking her knuckles.

He took her hand, examined the reddened fingers,
then eyed her quizzically. 'Shall I kiss it better?'

'Certainly not!' Ellis snatched her hand away then
marched back into the office. 'Now please let me get
on, Mr Canning. Maybe you don't have a home to
go to, but I do. And I like to see it occasionally.'

'As you know very well,' he said, following her, 'at
present I live in a hotel. A home is something I'm
working on.'

Ellis had no intention of showing interest in Matt Canning's personal life. 'I wish you success,' she said shortly.

'Wait a minute!' He barred her way. 'Have you something—or someone—to rush home to?'

'Yes,' lied Ellis. 'But since you saw fit to alter the arrangements without letting me know I'd better make sure everything's ready for the decorators before I go.'

'I'll help.' Matt was as good as his word. By the time the painters arrived with ladders and dustsheets his office was bare of everything bar three locked filing-cabinets which the men assured him they'd move out into the corridor on the trolley brought for the purpose.

'Thank you,' said Matt as they went down in the lift together. 'Sorry to rope you in for some heavy stuff, but I didn't fancy trusting my new desk to those chaps. That top is a slab of very expensive walnut.'

'You could have fooled me,' said Ellis bitterly. 'It felt like lead!'

'I hope you didn't wrench any muscles,' he remarked, as they emerged into the bright sunshine of a warm June evening.

'I don't think so. Have no fear—I'll be fit for work on Monday morning as usual!'

He paused halfway across the empty car park. 'That, my dear Miss Worth, was not what I meant.'

Ellis eyed him sceptically. 'Wasn't it, Mr Canning?'

The sun struck gleams of fire from his hair as Matt Canning smiled at her with rare warmth in his eyes. 'Am I such a slave-driver then, Ellis?'

She shrugged. 'I don't mind hard work, Mr Canning. And even if I did there's light at the end of the tunnel. By the end of August I'll be gone.'

'So you will.' Matt looked at her speculatively, then gestured at the glorious evening, at the sun still high above the trees lining the streets beyond the car park. 'I hate the thought of going back to the hotel on a night like this. Ellis, I know only too well I've been working you damned hard. Will you let me atone by taking you somewhere for a meal? I know a nice little pub by the river about ten miles or so west of Pennington.'

Ellis opened her mouth to refuse, then hesitated, tempted. The alternative was a sandwich or a salad on her little balcony. Alone. And tonight, for some indefinable reason, she felt like company. Male company at that. 'I said I had someone to go home to,' she reminded him.

'So you did.' He shrugged. 'I hoped against hope you were lying.'

She sighed. 'I was.'

He grinned, shaking an admonitory finger at her. 'Remember what happened to Pinocchio!'

She squinted her nose. 'It was a *white* lie. Anyway, my nose is still the same shape.'

'And a very nice one, too—well?' he added. 'Will you come?'

Ellis gazed at him thoughtfully, then shrugged. 'All right, but only if you give me time to change. I can't go out feeling hot and horrible the way I do now.'

'Right.' He shot back his shirt cuff to look at his watch. 'If I pick you up about eight does that give you enough time?'

CHAPTER FOUR

WHEN the Lotus arrived in Sycamore Road on the stroke of eight Ellis was not only ready, but waiting outside in the garden.

Matt sprang out of the car, looking different, more approachable, in fawn cords and a white shirt, with a rather elderly-looking cricket sweater knotted round his shoulders.

'Miraculous!' he said, striding towards her. 'A punctual woman.'

Ellis smiled, keeping quiet about the fact that she'd rushed like mad to be outside waiting. Allowing Charles's usurper across her own threshold had smacked too much of disloyalty for her taste. 'I'm always punctual,' she assured him.

'I don't doubt it.' He handed her into the car. 'Though a man could be forgiven for thinking it took hours to effect such a transformation. You're a delight to the eye, Ellis.'

She was glad to hear it, any doubts about the informality of her white-striped beige shirt and white linen trousers dispelled after seeing Matt. Not that her choice of clothes had been in the least haphazard. For some reason it had seemed important to look as different as possible from the tailored, efficient Miss Worth seen every day at Colcraft.

'You haven't forgotten I'm a nervous passenger?' she reminded him as they set off.

'Why does one look at my car convince everyone I'm some kind of maniac?' he complained, laughing. 'I promise I'll get you there and back in one piece, Ellis. After all,' he said, with a sly, headlong glance, 'as you said yourself, I need you back at your post on Monday.'

'So you do!'

'On the other hand, now the subject's come up, let's forget work and everything connected with it, just for a little while at least.'

'Amen to that.'

Once they'd left Pennington, Matt turned off on a meandering, minor road which led them through Gloucestershire countryside as beautiful as a painting in the soft sunset light. And now she was out with Matt Canning, away from Colcraft and all its hassle, Ellis found she was enjoying herself. Which, she told herself ironically, was hardly surprising. She would enjoy a gorgeous summer evening like this with any presentable companion who took her out into the country to dinner. It knocked spots off the solitary evening she'd faced as an alternative.

The pub Matt drove her to was called the Trout Inn, an unpretentious place hidden from the road in a fold in the hillside. A trout stream actually flowed through a garden dotted with tables where relaxed parents chatted under umbrellas as they watched their children throwing a ball for a red setter.

'Rufus belongs to the pub,' said Matt, as he led the way inside the crowded building.

'You know the place well?' Ellis asked, as he made a path for her through the packed, low-ceilinged rooms. 'Crumbs,' she added, as she wriggled her way through the crowd in his wake. 'Are we likely to get a meal tonight?'

'I booked it,' he said briefly, as the landlord beckoned them through into a small dining-room which, like the rest of the pub, was full, except for a table set for two in an alcove with a small window looking out on the stream at the back of the building.

'How did you manage this?' Ellis enquired with respect, once they were left alone to study the menus. 'You didn't ask me until after seven. I'd have thought this was completely booked by then.'

'I've been here quite a bit lately.' He shrugged. 'I like to get out of Pennington at weekends. I sometimes stay the night on a Saturday, spend most of Sunday here. The owners are pleasant people. They did some juggling when I rang asking for a table.'

Ellis eyed him quizzically over the top of the menu. 'Besides, you're not the type people say no to, are you?'

He shrugged. 'Not much, except for you, of course. I had to resort to base methods to prevent you walking out on me, remember.'

'Oh, I remember!' Her eyes flashed with resentment she made no attempt to hide.

He studied her for a moment. 'I wouldn't have carried out my threat, you know. I'm actually not such an unprincipled bastard that I'd have refused a reference if you'd really been dead set on leaving there and then.'

'Then why,' she whispered fiercely, leaning across the table, 'did you say you would?'

Matt hesitated a moment, then shrugged. 'Basically because I knew life would be easier for me with you on hand during my running-in period as MD. So I made sure you stayed.'

She eyed him coldly. 'You're unscrupulous. And there's nothing to stop me walking out on you on Monday, now I know the truth.'

'I realise that,' he said soberly. 'But I sincerely hope you won't. Not until the time specified, anyway.' His eyes met hers. 'Not that I think you will.'

'What makes you so sure?'

'Instinct.'

'I shouldn't bank on yours too much,' she retorted acidly, then took herself in hand. This was, after all, a social occasion, of a sort. One she might have done better to refuse, it was true, but since she hadn't it was only good manners to be polite, even pleasant. She managed a smile. 'The next time you ask me to heave furniture around I might pick up my traps and never darken Colcraft's door again.'

He captured her hand, his long forefinger gentle as he smoothed it over her reddened knuckles. 'I'm sorry about that, Ellis. I swear I won't ask you to lift anything heavier than a pen in future.'

Ellis pulled her hand away, annoyed to find herself flustered by the contact. She took refuge behind the large menu. 'I thought we agreed to forget work, anyway,' she said gruffly. 'What do you recommend to eat?' She looked up to meet an oddly disquieting look in his eyes. 'What's the matter?'

'Nothing,' he said absently, then applied himself to the menu. 'The chef's a genius with salmon, and of course the trout's good, but I can recommend most things.'

The meal was everything he'd promised. They both chose salmon, the speciality of the day, but Ellis refused a first course while they waited.

'I adore sinful puddings,' she confessed. 'But if I eat a first course I won't have room for one.'

Matt laughed. 'You look as though you never eat anything sinful at all—as though you live on fresh fruit and yoghurt with never an additive in sight.'

'Why?' she asked lightly. 'Do I look so very plain and wholesome, then?'

'Wholesome, yes. Plain, quite definitely not.' He raised his glass to her. 'What shall we drink to?'

'*Détente*, perhaps?'

'Excellent—to *détente* by all means!'

As the evening wore on Ellis found she needed to remind herself every now and then that this was Matthew Canning, usurper of Charles Longman's rightful throne, by no means just an interesting and attentive male escort. It would also be prudent to remember that this was the man she would face across his back-breaking walnut desk come Monday morning, that the smile she found so disarming at this very moment could change in the twinkling of an eye, as she knew only too well, to the smile on the face of the tiger.

While she was rhapsodising over coffee soufflé with caramel sauce Matt reintroduced the subject of his plans for somewhere to live.

'I've put in a bid for a house in a village about seven miles or so the other side of Pennington,' he said, spreading ripe Stilton on a biscuit. 'It's a place called Nether Combe. Do you know it?'

Ellis almost choked on her last spoonful of pudding. Nether Combe was only a couple of miles down the road from Briar Cottage. 'Er—yes. I know it. Very picturesque. Have you by any chance bought the Old Rectory?'

'Good lord, how did you know that?'

'I—I saw it was up for sale in the paper. When are you moving in?'

He sighed. 'Next week—if I live that long. Tonight I feel rather less than enthusiastic at the prospect of humping furniture and emptying tea-chests.'

'Well, don't look at me! My experience earlier this evening was quite enough in that line.'

'Pity,' he said, grinning, then went on with some enthusiasm to describe his new home, which he forecast would take up every last minute of spare time at his disposal for the foreseeable future. 'I'm mad, I suppose,' he added, shaking his head, 'but the minute I set foot through the door I was hooked.'

'Not so mad,' said Ellis practically. 'Property's always an investment, especially if you intend doing the place up.'

They went on talking in a leisurely, unexpectedly easy way over coffee until Ellis realised with surprise that they were the only people left in the dining-room. The Friday night rush was over.

'It must be time we went, Mr Canning.'

'Don't say that!'

Ellis looked at him in surprise. 'I'm sure they want to clear up, and frankly, much as I've enjoyed the evening, I'm beginning to flag. I don't wish to offend you and all that, but I've had a very hard day.'

He got up to hold her chair for her. 'I meant it sounds ludicrous for you to keep calling me "Mr Canning" under these circumstances. I answer very happily to Matt.'

'That, of course,' she said as they went out into the now deserted garden, 'is out of the question.'

Matt paused as they reached the car. 'Why? I use your first name.'

She sighed impatiently. 'That's irrelevant. Except for Miss Morrison secretaries at Colcraft are all known by their first names. But not one of them has ever been on the same terms with the men they work for.'

'I meant socially.'

Ellis stiffened. 'This evening was a one-off, Mr Canning. I came because I was tempted by the prospect of a delicious meal in a pretty place on a lovely evening like this. And, most important of all,' she added bitingly, 'I said yes because my job with you is temporary. If it were permanent I'd have refused point-blank.'

He leaned against the car, his expression hidden from her in the dim light. 'Are you saying that in all the years you worked for Longman he never took you out for a meal—even when you worked late?'

'That's exactly what I'm saying,' she said coldly, her pleasure in the evening spoilt. 'Now, Mr Canning, if you don't mind I'd like to get home.'

He opened the passenger door for her in a silence which prevailed unbroken during the long journey back to Pennington. But when they arrived in Sycamore Road Matt leapt from the car to open Ellis's door for her, his hand on her wrist to stay her when she tried to brush past.

'Look, Ellis, I'm sorry if I offended you.'

'Oh, but you didn't!' She gave him a bright, impersonal smile. 'Thank you for the meal. I can't think why I've never heard of the Trout Inn before. It's a delightful place.' She tried in vain to pull her hand away, furious to find herself flustered again at the warm, strong pressure of it.

'Something tells me,' he said softly, pulling her nearer, 'that this may be the only opportunity I'll ever have.'

'For what?' she demanded, trying to free herself.

'You can't be that naïve, Ellis Worth.' He wrapped his arms round her, looking down into her eyes for the last second before his mouth met hers, then his arms tightened convulsively as electricity, sudden and unexpected, flared between them like summer lightning, fusing them together in sudden, flooding need which rendered them oblivious to everything else around them until a car turned into Sycamore Road, bringing them back to earth. Ellis jumped away, breathing raggedly, her eyes dazed and incredulous as they met the heat in Matt's. He moved after her, purpose in every line of him, but she shook her head violently, took to her heels and fled from him round to the back of the house, racing up the stairs to her flat in unreasoning panic.

With her door locked safely behind her, Ellis rushed to open all her windows to the night air, her blood still pounding through her veins. What a fool she'd been to go out with Matt Canning in the first place! She should have known he'd expect some return for the meal once they got home. He was still convinced, of course, that similar arrangements with Charles Longman had been a way of life for her. Which was a joke. She'd worked late for Charles Longman more times than she'd had hot dinners, but he'd never bought one for her! Nor had his one, fleeting little kiss been in the least like the heated exchange with

Matt Canning just now—which had been in full view of anyone passing, too, she realised, her face on fire.

She paced through her small domain like a restless tigress, disgusted with her mindless response to a man who probably thought she'd been having an affair with Charles Longman all along. Whereas the truth couldn't have been more different. All the years she'd been in love with Charles she'd never really thought of him in terms of—of bed. Her worship of him had been infinitely more cerebral. Certainly nothing like the way she'd felt tonight when Matt kissed her. She shuddered, thankful they'd been outside, no matter who'd been looking on. If she'd let Matt into her flat the incident might have had a very different conclusion, one which gave Ellis the most restless night of her life as she tried in vain not to think about it.

Ellis spent the rest of the weekend at Briar Cottage, so *distraite* most of the time that her mother and aunt, though refraining from comment, were worried. Ellis, too immersed in depression to notice for once, spent most of her time in the garden, helping her aunt with the mowing and weeding, pastimes which left her mind free to grapple with her various problems. The solution to the main one was obvious—she would just have to hand Matt her notice first thing Monday morning, even if it did mean joining the ranks of the unemployed. She couldn't possibly go on working for him under the circumstances. Her decision made, Ellis forced herself to dismiss Matt Canning from her mind, and went indoors to scour the appointments sections of the newspapers her mother had brought from the local newsagent. Her search, Ellis found to her gloom, yielded nothing remotely possible in the Pennington area.

'All the tempting jobs are in London,' she sighed over Sunday lunch.

'Do you fancy moving there?' asked her mother, trying to hide her dismay.

'No, I don't. Why should I tear myself away from you and all my friends at my age? Besides, I've almost finished paying off the mortgage on my flat.'

To change the subject, she surprised her loved ones by informing them that the new managing director had bought a house in Nether Combe.

'Did you tell him we lived nearby?' asked Lydia.

'No fear. I like my private life to myself, Auntie, dear!'

After supper that evening Polly summoned Ellis from the washing-up to the telephone. 'A man,' she announced. 'Wouldn't give his name.'

Ellis stiffened. Surely Matt Canning wouldn't have the effrontery to contact her here?

'Ellis Worth,' she announced belligerently.

'Hi, there. It's Charles.'

The unmistakable drawl took her breath away. Ellis sat down with a bump on an oak settle. 'Why, Mr Longman——'

'Oh, come on, Ellis. No need for all that rot any more. Just call me Charles!'

Not Charlie?

'How did you find me?' she asked.

'I rang your flat, but no joy, then I remembered you stayed most weekends at your aunt's place and did a bit of detective work.' He sounded very pleased with himself.

'How are you? Is all going well at CCS?'

There was a pause. 'Actually, that's what I'm ringing about. I wondered if we might meet.'

Ellis's eyes widened. Meet? 'Charles—is there something wrong?'

'No, no. I've just had this brainwave, that's all. Got something to put to you. How about dinner Tuesday night?'

Ellis stared at the phone, dumbfounded.

'Ellis?' repeated Charles impatiently. 'Are you there?'

'Yes—yes, I'm here.'

'I must talk to you—urgently. I need your help, Ellis.'

When she hesitated for a moment Charles repeated his plea coaxingly.

'Don't say no, there's a darling.'

How men hated the word 'no', thought Ellis. 'All right,' she said, at last. 'Where shall I meet you?'

'I could come and pick you up——'

'No,' she said quickly. 'I'll drive into town.'

'Right. See you in the bar of the Chesterton sevenish, then. Thanks, Ellis, you're a star.'

After he'd rung off Ellis sat very still, staring through the open door into the garden. Her feelings were mixed. What on earth could Charles want? It had to be something pretty urgent for him to offer her dinner!

Ellis got so little sleep back in her flat that night that she gave up soon after first light, deciding to pamper herself with a leisurely breakfast in the cool early morning air. At first she was tempted to ring in to say she was ill, but thought better of it. It would only postpone her first meeting with Matt, not avoid it.

After her weekend in the sun her skin was tanned a smooth olive-gold, and for once Ellis rebelled at the thought of her usual tailored suits. Instead she put on a thin dress of burnt orange cotton, a shade which flattered her. She looked, she knew, very different from the usual super-efficient Miss Worth, and was pleased. If the day proved trying, and no doubt it would, her frivolous dress would serve as a comforting reminder that her days as the managing director's secretary were numbered.

When she arrived in the Colcraft car park it was so early that she was first there, as once she had always been. Matt's parking space was empty. Relieved, Ellis made good use of the respite before Matt's arrival. She was soon so absorbed in her task of editing and printing the minutes left from Friday that his buzzer was her first intimation that Matt Canning was in the building. Ellis finished her current page without haste, then went through into the managing director's office, the smell of fresh paint a reminder that she must comment on the changes. She smiled politely at Matt as she greeted him, waving a hand at walls painted a soft mushroom shade.

'Very nice.'

'I'm glad you approve,' he said shortly. 'But I didn't get you in here to discuss interior decoration.'

'Very well, Mr Canning.' Ellis sat down, notebook in hand. 'Are you ready to make a start?'

He was silent for a moment, his eyes unwavering on her face, the dark-rimmed irises glittering like ice. 'There's a letter missing from this lot,' he said at last, indicating the pile in front of him.

'Really?' Ellis jumped up. 'Tell me what it is and I'll chase it up.'

'Sit down.'

She resumed her chair without haste, smoothing down the bright cotton of her skirt.

'The document I'm referring to,' he went on with deliberation, 'is your letter of resignation.'

'You can have it if you want.'

'You bloody well know I don't want it,' he said irritably. 'But after what happened on Friday night——'

'Mr Canning, I've put Friday night from my mind,' she said firmly. 'I quite understand that you gave in to a sudden impulse. I don't hold it against you. In fact I blame myself. I should never have consented to an evening out with you in the first place. It probably misled you regarding what to expect afterwards by way of thanks.'

He glared at her. 'I expected nothing, Ellis. My intention was a mere friendly peck on your cheek to apologise for my reference to Charles Longman. That it turned out differently was as much a surprise to me as to you.'

Ellis nodded matter-of-factly. 'I see. Let's forget it, then. Incidentally,' she added, 'the reason you don't have my notice this morning is my passion for security. Over the weekend I had, as you expected, made up my mind to leave. But in the cold light of day this morning I realised I can't afford such a dramatic gesture. To keep paying off my mortgage I must have another job in view before I leave Colcraft.'

Matt relaxed almost imperceptibly. 'Nothing yet?' he asked.

'No.' She smiled a little. 'But I'm looking. Perhaps you could keep an ear to the ground for something suitable, Mr Canning. You must have a great many contacts.'

'I do,' he agreed, suddenly dangerously affable, 'but why should I assist in depriving myself of an efficient assistant like you, Ellis?'

'I'm your secretary, not your assistant, Mr Canning.'

'But if you were, with a suitable rise in salary,' he pounced, 'would you consider working for me on a permanent basis?'

Ellis shook her head decisively. 'I'm afraid not, Mr Canning.'

He shrugged. 'Yet you must admit we work well together.' He gave her a bright, speculative look. 'I thought we socialised rather well together, too.'

She smiled sweetly. 'Not, I'm sure, that you intended repeating the occasion, but if I were to accept permanent employment with you, Mr Canning, it would rule out further socialising anyway. I make it a rule never to fraternise with the man I work for. Contrary,' she said bitingly, 'to your belief regarding Mr Longman and myself.'

'To hell with Longman,' he snapped. 'Right. Enough time wasted, I think. Let's get on.'

Matthew Canning drove himself, and Ellis, to the point of exhaustion all through that day and the next, so that by the time she was ready to leave on Tuesday Ellis was in no mood to dine with Charles or anyone else.

Matt looked up at her, eyes narrowed, when she went in to ask if she could leave the rest of the report she was typing until next day.

'Got something on tonight?' he enquired, rising from his seat.

Ellis flushed. 'Yes, as a matter of fact.'

'Have fun, then.'

'Goodnight,' she said stiffly, turning away, only to collide with Matt, who'd moved to open the door for her. She stumbled, and he grabbed her by the elbows to steady her, breathing in sharply as his fingers closed on her bare skin. Ellis stared up into his dilated eyes in dismay, paralysed by the familiar heat rushing through her veins at his touch.

Matt let her go, slowly, as though his hands were reluctant to perform his brain's bidding. Ellis backed away from him like a sleepwalker, then the sound of voices in the corridor outside brought her back to life with a jolt, and she turned and fled from the room.

She drove home at twice her usual speed, hell-bent on putting as much distance between herself and Matt as possible. This, she told herself passionately, couldn't go on. She didn't like the man very much, resented him, even, yet one touch from him and she was reduced to jelly! And she wished now there were some way of contacting Charles to cancel this dinner-date, amazed to find she actually meant it as she parked the car in Sycamore Road. A few weeks ago the prospect of dinner with Charles would have transported her straight to cloud nine. Get yourself together, you idiot, she ordered herself fiercely.

But later, bathed and scented and arrayed in a slim linen dress the colour of strawberry ice-cream, Ellis found she was human enough to feel a *frisson* of anticipation after all as she parked her car behind the Chesterton Hotel. But she felt guilty, too. She knew quite well she should have refused to come. But the temptation of seeing Charles again had been too strong. As she entered the hotel she looked about her furtively, wishing Charles had chosen somewhere less popular than the Chesterton. But it was early for most diners. And there was no danger of running into Matt, she comforted herself. He'd mentioned earlier that he was picnicking at the Old Rectory this evening, making lists of everything he needed for the move at the weekend. To Ellis's relief Charles was the only one in the bar. He was chatting to the barman, looking suave and elegant, as always, in an expensive fawn suit. His handsome features lit with a smile as he saw Ellis. He came hurrying towards her, hand outstretched.

'My dear, how good to see you.'

'Hello.' She took his hand briefly, feeling oddly shy. 'How are you?'

He assured her he was in the pink, ushered her to a sofa in a corner, gave in with some teasing to her insistence on a soft drink, then to her surprise made no mention of the reason for the meeting, but kept up a stream of small talk while they chose their meal. Ellis eyed him closely as he consulted with the waiter, noting new lines at his eyes and mouth, a look of strain about him despite all the *bonhomie*. He asked how things were at Colcraft, and how she was getting on without him, and regaled her with a series of amusing anecdotes about his new job throughout the meal. They were at the coffee stage before Charles Longman abandoned the role of jovial host and got to grips with the real reason for his invitation.

'I feel very guilty about you, Ellis,' he said abruptly.

She eyed him questioningly as she poured coffee. 'Really? Why should you?'

'I was so taken up with my own woes when the balloon went up that I never gave a thought about what you were going to do once I left.'

He was honest, anyway, thought Ellis wryly. 'I'm fine,' she assured him. 'You've no need to worry about *me*.'

'But I do!' Charles leaned forward across the table to seize her hand. 'I admit I've been a self-centred swine, but I'm here to make reparation, Ellis.'

As she searched his face, wondering what he meant, Ellis recognised a familiar wheedling look in Charles's eyes which meant he needed a favour of some kind. And expected her to grant it. It saddened her. The pull of the old infatuation was still there to a certain extent. Perhaps it had been too much of a way of life for too long to disappear altogether, but it contained an element of nostalgia now. Once she would have been in seventh heaven to be dining here with Charles. Now she found to her dismay that she felt merely uncomfortable, filled with a sensation of uneasiness which increased by the minute. She withdrew her hand sharply. 'There's nothing to make reparation for, Charles. Truly. I'm fine.'

'But I heard your job with Canning isn't permanent,' he said, frowning. 'Why not, for Pete's sake? The man must be mad.'

'But Charles——'

'No, Ellis. Don't say a word. Just listen! Brandy?'

'No, nothing, thanks.'

'Then listen to my proposition,' he ordered. 'How about coming to work for me at CCS?'

Ellis stared at him in astonishment. 'But surely you have a secretary, Charles!'

His eyes slid away from hers. 'Well, yes I have. But she's useless. No initiative, no personality; the woman's just a piece of office furniture. I need someone who can think for herself, someone with brains, who can be my right hand. In short, *you*,' he added, with a coaxing smile. 'I never realised how much I'd miss you, Ellis. I heard on the grapevine that your job with Canning was only temporary, so I had this brainwave. Come and work for me at CCS!'

'But Charles,' said Ellis gently, 'it's fifty miles away.'

He looked blank. 'What difference does that make?'

'I live in Pennington. I've bought my own flat here—and I dislike driving. I couldn't possibly drive there and back every day.'

Charles stared at her, puzzled. 'Nonsense! Of course you could.' He shrugged. 'But if not you could move, Ellis. Get a flat near CCS.'

Hurt and exasperated, Ellis was seized with a sudden, burning desire to go home. She shook her head impatiently. 'I don't want to move. I like my home, and I like being near my family.' She looked up, then froze, her eyes dilating in sudden horror as she saw Matt standing in the doorway, his eyes searching the room. 'Oh, no!' she said in a strangled voice.

'What's the matter?' Charles twisted around in his chair, his face like thunder as he recognised the tall figure striding towards them. 'What the hell do *you* want?' he said angrily, as Matt slid into one of the empty chairs to join them. 'Hell's bells, Canning,' he spluttered, but Matt silenced him with a look of such icy rage that Ellis quailed.

'Shut up, Longman, and listen,' he said in a furious undertone. 'I've just had a phone call from Clarissa.'

'*Clarissa!*' Charles went white.

'Yes, Clarissa. Your wife, should you need reminding. She's on her way into Pennington at this moment. She rang me up in a raging temper, saying she was sure you were meeting someone here tonight, and she was pretty sure she knew who it was.' Matt looked at Ellis coldly. 'She told me it was you.'

Charles groaned, his hands shaking as he beckoned to the waiter. 'I've got to get out of here,' he muttered hoarsely, fumbling for his wallet. 'How long ago did she ring?'

'I'd say you've got twenty minutes' grace unless she breaks the sound barrier,' said Matt tersely. 'When you've paid the three of us are going to walk out of here quietly, smiling at anyone we know on the way, then I advise you to drive like a bat out of hell while Ellis and I have a drink in the bar.'

'I'm going to do no such thing——' began Ellis, but Matt silenced her with a look, as the waiter came to take the money Charles almost hurled at him in his hurry to get away.

Every nerve in her body crawling with tension, Ellis walked with the two men at a pace which seemed like a funeral march, any attempt to quicken it up foiled by Matt's fingers biting into her elbow to hold her back. Once outside in the foyer, Charles muttered a hasty goodnight then took to his heels to sprint for his car.

'Let's have a drink,' said Matt, his grip like iron as he steered Ellis into the dimly lit cocktail bar. He settled her in a corner on the same sofa she'd shared with Charles earlier, then ordered two brandies from the waiter, before looking questioningly at Ellis. 'Are you all right?'

'No, I'm not all right!' She shrank away as he moved closer. 'This is like a French farce. I want to go home. Now.'

'You can't. I told Clarissa she'd got hold of the wrong end of the stick—that you couldn't be dining with Charles because you were meeting me for a drink.' He took hold of her hand, leaning over her in parody of an enamoured consort. 'She didn't believe a word of it. So when she comes tearing in here like an avenging angel she must find you and me together, apparently talking shop. I said we had some business problems to discuss. No time in work and so on.'

'And she believed that?'

'You'd better hope she did!' Matt's eyes were scathing. 'So this is what you were in such a hurry to get to tonight. Were you out of your mind, meeting Charles here at the Chesterton?'

Ellis dropped her eyes, flushing with mortification. 'He was—persuasive,' she said jerkily, after a welcome interruption from the waiter with their drinks.

'No doubt. Drink your brandy,' he ordered.

'I loathe brandy!'

'Drink it just the same. It'll steady your nerves.'

Ellis took a deep breath then downed the brandy as if it were medicine, coughing as the fiery spirit took her breath away.

'I didn't mean drink it down in one go,' he said impatiently.

'My nerves feel worse now!' she gasped.

'I'm not surprised. Lean against me.' He slid his arm round her shoulders. Ellis tensed, but the arm tightened. She flung her head back to object then stiffened as she met a pair of cold blue eyes. Clarissa

Longman stood watching them, a baffled look of disbelief on her face.

'Well, well,' she said tightly. 'Good evening to you both. So you weren't lying, Matt.'

'Now would I do that?' he countered lightly, getting up. 'What can I get you to drink?'

Clarissa sat down with a sigh of angry frustration. 'I suppose a gin and tonic won't affect the drive home. I'd have been here earlier but I got held up only yards from the house. A haywain had overturned in the lane, would you believe? I couldn't get out of my own drive.'

Ellis felt a surge of gratitude for the driver of the haywain.

'No point in beating about the bush,' Clarissa went on bitterly. 'I might as well tell you the truth, Ellis. I thought Charles was here with you. I wouldn't believe Matt when he said you were meeting *him*. Frankly I'd have sworn you'd be too loyal to Charles to hitch your wagon to the new star.'

Ellis felt dizzy, both from the brandy and the adrenalin which had been pumping through her veins since the minute she'd seen Matt.

'Whereas,' said Matt, arriving back with Clarissa's drink, 'we were about to leave when you arrived. We poor fools have to get up in the morning, you know.'

'Together?' asked Clarissa acidly.

'Certainly not,' snapped Ellis, before Matt could say a word. 'I merely *work* for Mr Canning. Which is all I ever did for Mr Longman, too. Until tonight.'

Matt impaled her with a warning look.

She ignored him. 'Actually, you were quite right, Mrs Longman. Your husband did ask me to dinner here tonight. But not for the reasons you suspected. It was all perfectly innocent and above board.'

Clarissa Longman looked taken aback. She eyed the anger in Matt's face, registered it, then turned back to Ellis. 'You're honest, anyway! What were these innocent reasons, may I ask?'

'You may, but I can't answer. If you want to know you must ask Mr Longman yourself.'

'Always the perfect confidential secretary,' said Clarissa cuttingly.

'Which is all I've ever been,' Ellis assured her.

Clarissa looked unconvinced, then turned to Matt, her ice-blue eyes wide and speculative. 'So why, I wonder, did you lie? Why did you tell me you were the one Ellis was meeting?'

He shrugged, his face inscrutable now. 'Because I knew you were barking up the wrong tree, Clarissa. Ellis isn't the one you want.'

CHAPTER FIVE

WHEN the car drew up in Sycamore Road Matt jumped out quickly to steady Ellis as she scrambled clumsily to the pavement.

'It was kind of you to drive me home,' she said politely.

'I could hardly let you drive. One brandy seemed to knock you for six. Did you have much wine with your meal?'

'Only one glass. Charles insisted.'

'Charles,' observed Matt abrasively, as he steered her up the steps to her balcony, 'has a lot to answer for. Anyway, the shock knocked you for six, not the alcohol. I'd like to knock that bloody fool's teeth down his throat. What did he think he was playing at—taking you to the Chesterton of all places?'

To her embarrassment Ellis had difficulty fitting her key into the lock. After a moment or two Matt relieved her of it, then followed her into her small sitting-room, ready, she realised, to catch her if she fell.

'You're a ghastly colour,' he informed her.

Ellis felt her stomach lurch, swallowed hard, then fled for the bathroom, where she parted with the brandy, the coffee and—by the way she felt when the spasm was over—everything she'd eaten for days. For a minute or two she sat in a huddle on the bathroom floor, then dragged herself to her feet. She washed

'Of course not,' said Ellis scathingly. 'At least, not about me. The gist of his discourse was quite the reverse from "come live with me and be my love." He was simply offering me a job.'

'You mean the bastard can't cope at CCS without you to nanny for him again, I suppose!' He eyed her narrowly. 'What did you say?'

Ellis hugged her arms across her chest, looking away. 'I told him I couldn't travel that far every day—or move from Pennington, as he suggested.'

Matt surveyed her in silence for a while. 'I never really believed I'd find you with Longman tonight, you know,' he said at last.

'It was all perfectly innocent,' she said drearily. 'After all,' she added, looking up to meet his eyes at last, 'who in his right mind would choose the Chesterton for a clandestine little dinner? Charles keeps to out-of-the-way places a long way from home for that kind of thing.'

Matt's face hardened into granite. 'How do you know that?'

'Because I made the bookings for him, of course! I used to send flowers and little presents for him afterwards, too. But I've never told a soul before. I shouldn't now,' she said quickly in remorse. 'Especially you. I suppose you'll rush off to report it all to Clarissa.'

His eyes filled with disgust. 'What the hell do you think I am? On the other hand,' he added slowly, his eyes holding hers, 'I might possibly do that if you tell me the name of the woman in question.'

Ellis glared at him, incensed. 'How magnanimous do you expect me to be, for heaven's sake? Charles is no plaster saint, as I know better than anyone. But he was always very kind to me. We got on well together. We had a very good working relationship—and I use the word "working" very deliberately. There's such a thing as loyalty, you know! She's no friend of mine. Whereas Charles was. Is,' she amended hastily, then gave Matt a disenchanted little smile. 'Besides, Charles always believed in safety in numbers. There's a long list of names. But as far as I'm concerned Clarissa Longman can whistle for it!' She hugged her arms across her chest, feeling cold. 'Look, I'm very grateful for your help tonight, but would you mind leaving now? I'm terribly tired.'

'Not before I make you some tea and toast,' Matt said firmly. 'You look like a ghost.'

'I don't want anything——'

'Well, *I* do. I missed dinner to rush to your aid, remember.'

Ellis, although all she longed for was solitude, had no option but to make him a snack, toasting several slices of bread she served with some of her mother's mushroom pâté. She made a pot of coffee which she shared with him once she'd repaired some of the ravages made by her tears.

'I know you're wishing me anywhere in the world but where I am,' observed Matt as he wolfed the impromptu meal.

'Not at all,' she said politely. 'It was the least I could do after your knight errantry.' She poured more coffee in their cups, looking at him curiously. 'You and Clarissa are obviously old friends.'

He shook his head. 'Not really. The link between us is the girl I shared a flat with in college. Clarissa was an old school-friend of Laura's, which is how I came to meet her.'

After that, by tacit consent, they abandoned personal talk. Matt, in an effort to return to normal, changed the subject to talk about Colcraft affairs and Ellis found her interest caught, despite her depression, as he told her about various changes he had in the pipeline.

'A pity,' he said after a while, 'that you won't be round to see them implemented.'

'True.' Ellis felt a sharp pang at the thought. 'But after tonight it's going to be difficult to go on working for you as though nothing had happened. At the moment I feel too numb to care, but I know perfectly well I'll wake up in the morning—always supposing I ever get to sleep tonight—unable to look you in the face again. It's a habit of mine lately.'

'That's silly,' he said brusquely. 'Things will look different in the morning. We just go on as though tonight never happened.'

'Easier said than done!' Ellis got to her feet, stacking plates on the tray.

'Let me take that in for you.' Matt took the tray to her minuscule kitchen, then turned to confront her. Involuntarily Ellis backed away.

'Don't,' he said very quietly. 'My intention was merely to thank you for the coffee. I'll expect you bright and early in the morning, with all this nonsense put behind you.'

'Yes. Of course. Goodnight—and thank you again.' She turned away quickly to show him to the door, standing back to let him pass through.

Matt put out a hand to touch her cheek. 'Sleep well.'

Ellis stood very still beneath the caress. Her mouth dried as she saw his eyes change, the dark rims widening to blot out the silvery irises as his hand moved with infinite care along the line of her jaw, sliding to the nape of her neck as he bent his head very slowly until his lips rested on hers. She leaned against him like a tired child, finding comfort in the security of his arms at first. But the numb feeling quickly ebbed away. In its place the now familiar tide of heat came surging through her veins and she gasped, and his mouth hardened in response, his arms closing round her like steel bands as his tongue sought hers with a demand which brought her to earth with a bump. Ellis uttered a strangled little sound, shying away as though she'd been scalded.

'I'm sorry,' he said hoarsely. 'I didn't intend——'

'I know, I know!' She looked at him beseechingly. 'Please go now.'

Matt stood, tense, for a moment, then shrugged. He turned away without another word and let himself out of the flat, leaving Ellis a prey to so many mixed emotions that she made no attempt to sort them out as she stripped off her clothes to stand in the shower for a long, long time before crawling into bed.

Next morning, looking fit and vital as always, Matthew Canning gave Ellis no time to feel embarrassed when she arrived. He asked her briskly how she was feeling, then got down to business in a way which made it plain that personalities were to provide no obstacle to the smooth running of Colcraft. Ellis followed his lead with alacrity, grateful for the daunting pile of work he left her to get on with before he took off on a surprise inspection of one of the subsidiary companies under his aegis.

The rest of the week was hectic in the extreme, but went by without any complications of an emotional nature, other than Matt's ill-concealed irritability when Ellis asked him for a day off the following Monday to attend an interview for a new job.

'You're determined to desert me, then?' he asked as they were finishing up for the weekend.

'I always told you I'd leave at the end of August.'

'Where's the interview?' he demanded, watching from the doorway as she put her office to rights with her usual meticulous care.

'Just outside Gloucester.'

'I thought you didn't care for travelling.'

'I don't. I'd prefer something nearer, I admit.' She shrugged. 'Time enough to worry about that if I'm offered the job.'

'Of course you'll be offered the job!' He looked at his watch. 'I'd better get cracking if I'm to be at Nether Combe before the removal people.'

'I'd forgotten that—good luck with the move.'

'How are you spending the weekend?'

'Brushing up on company law before the interview. It was my weak spot when I qualified.'

Matt's eyes narrowed. 'What *is* this job you're after?'

'The post is described as secretary to the company secretary. It's an engineering group.' Ellis shrugged. 'The successful applicant, as they say, could in the fullness of time reach the dizzy heights of company secretary him or herself.'

He rubbed his chin thoughtfully. 'Is that what you want?'

'Why else do you think I studied with the Chartered Institute of Secretaries and Administrators, Mr Canning?' She slung the strap of her handbag over her shoulder, smiling. 'Or maybe you don't approve of female company secretaries.'

'Frankly, I'd never given the idea much thought. I suppose I'd better wish you good luck then, Ellis.'

She nodded jauntily. 'Thank you, Mr Canning. I'll work late on Tuesday if necessary to make up.'

The interview was exhausting but challenging. On the whole Ellis felt she'd acquitted herself well, and drove back to Pennington in high spirits.

'You look very pleased with yourself,' commented Matt the next day. 'I take it the interview went well.'

'Very well. It's always difficult to say, of course, but I think I stand a good chance.' Ellis smiled philosophically. 'I'm not worried. If they turn me down there'll be other jobs.'

'You *could* keep working for me,' he said, rolling a pen between his fingers.

'No, I couldn't,' she said firmly.

'Why? Because you're afraid I'll pounce on you and ravish you on my new office carpet?'

Ellis flushed scarlet. 'Certainly not!'

'Liar.' His eyes locked with hers. 'Your brain may not like me very much, Ellis Worth, and I know damn well you resent the fact that I got the job instead of Charles Longman, but...' He paused deliberately, smiling in a way which put her teeth on edge. 'But there have been certain indications that in other ways we are very compatible.'

'There'll be no more,' she snapped, willing her colour to subside. 'I'll be gone, soon.'

'Are you so eager to leave?'

Ellis paused, her anger subsiding. 'I'm not eager to leave Colcraft at all,' she admitted, thinking it over. 'I was very happy here until...'

'Until Longman left and I arrived,' he said shortly. 'So if you hadn't been obliged to work for me personally you'd have been quite happy to stay, I take it?'

'Yes,' she said baldly. 'Perfectly happy. But under the circumstances it's best I go as soon as I'm successful with a new post. Shall I advise Personnel to advertise for a replacement?'

'Leave it until you know something definite.' He pulled a folder towards him. 'I'm afraid there's a lot left over from yesterday, so we'd better get on.'

Ellis hesitated, then took the plunge and asked him the question she'd been nerving herself to ask ever since the night she'd dined with Charles.

'Before we do would you mind telling me whether you've heard anything more from Mrs Longman? About her suspicions as far as I'm concerned,' she added uncomfortably.

'I have, as it happens,' he said coldly. 'She rang me a couple of days later—didn't I mention it?'

'You certainly did not!'

'Really?' He shrugged. 'Anyway, you're in the clear. Clarissa admitted freely she'd been wrong about you all along. Apparently she's discovered Charles is involved with a dashing divorcée by the name of Monica Caldwell. Ring any bells?'

She stared at him, incensed, her eyes spitting green sparks. 'You mean,' she said at last, 'that you've known for days that she believed what I said, yet you didn't bother to tell me?'

Matt shrugged. 'Let's say I felt you deserved to fry just a little. After all, you *were* dining with Charles that night. I thought a spot of old-fashioned remorse and fretting wouldn't do you any harm. It might even make you think a bit before you rush off to his aid if he asks again—as he probably will if Clarissa makes life difficult for him.'

Ellis said nothing, preserving a silence so stony that he turned away irritably in the end to address himself to the paperwork piling the desk between them.

From that day on Ellis preserved a vow of silence of a sort. She never addressed one word to Matthew Canning irrelevant to the affairs of Colcraft. If he mentioned anything else, from his move to his new house, to her own well-being, she merely changed the subject so flatly that the atmosphere in the newly decorated office rarely rose above freezing, despite the warm summer weather. As a means of reparation for his bloody-mindedness it was perfect. As the days passed Matt's irritability worsened by the hour, while Ellis remained cool and remote, never deviating by the flicker of an eyelash from the role of perfect secretary. The moments of intimacy between them might never have occurred.

It was an intolerable situation, but one she had no intention of improving. Every morning she waited eagerly for a reply from the engineering group, praying they would give her the job, but when the letter came it was merely to say that her name was on the shortlist for the post and could she present herself for a second interview?

'I shall need Tuesday off, please, Mr Canning,' she announced later, before they began on the business of the day.

He raised his head, his eyes cold with sarcasm.
'Wonders will never cease. The ice-maiden speaks.'

'There was no other way to ask for time off, Mr
Canning.'

'What for? Another job?'

'No, Mr Canning. A second interview for the same
one. I've been short-listed,' she said colourlessly.

Matt stared at her morosely for a moment, as
though waiting for her to say more, then shrugged
irritably. 'Very well. Mark the date down on my diary.'

'Yes, Mr Canning. Thank you.'

'If,' he said dangerously, leaning across the desk,
'you say Mr Canning once more this morning, I won't
answer for the consequences.'

Ellis ignored him, as she leaned across to make the
necessary note in his diary. But she flinched as her
hand touched his by accident, and he smiled evilly.

'Don't worry. I won't pounce on you—not right
now, anyway. It's too early in the day.'

But by now she was skilled at keeping her feelings
under control. Her face showed none of her deep satisfaction at the baffled look in his eyes as she re-
treated behind her screen of silence.

CHAPTER SIX

NEXT day Ellis was rather surprised when Brenda Harris, Godfrey Baker's secretary, asked her to spare a few minutes for Mr Baker after lunch. Ellis, intrigued, went straight to the company secretary's office after her lunch-hour, accepting his offer of tea as he waved her to a chair in front of his desk. Godfrey Baker chatted for a while as Ellis poured out, his eyes scrutinising her closely, plainly approving of what he saw. Since her war of silence with Matt Ellis she had reverted to her severity, and today was dressed in a clerical grey suit, with a white-dotted black bow tie at the collar of her white shirt.

She sipped her tea, eyeing him expectantly. 'Is there something I can do for you, Mr Baker?'

'I hear you're in line for a job elsewhere,' he answered obliquely. 'Matt tells me you're short-listed for a post with some engineering group.'

Annoyed to learn Matt Canning had been discussing her, Ellis nodded briefly. 'Yes, Mr Baker. The job with Mr Canning was never intended as anything more than a stop-gap.'

'You're annoyed because Matt told me?'

'And surprised, Mr Baker.'

'He had a purpose, so don't get on your high horse.' Godfrey Baker's shrewd eyes scrutinised her closely. 'Are you dead set on leaving Colcraft, Ellis?'

She sighed. 'No, I'm not. I shall be sorry in many ways. The company's been very good to me.'

'Then I have a suggestion to make,' he said briskly. 'Matt thinks you're wasted as a mere secretary.'

'There's nothing "mere" about being a secretary,' she retorted hotly. 'Believe me, with a man like Mr Canning it's dashed hard work.'

He smiled. 'In that case how would you like to work for me instead?'

Ellis stared at him. 'But Brenda——'

'Brenda, alas, is deserting me. She retires in a couple of weeks.'

'Oh, I'm sorry. I didn't know.' Ellis smiled sympathetically. 'You'll miss her.'

'I certainly will. So how about making an old man happy by working for me in her place?'

She stared at him doubtfully, unsure how to answer.

Godfrey Baker leaned forward in his seat, quite plainly enjoying himself. 'You have doubts, I see. In that case, Miss Ellis Worth, let me dangle a very juicy carrot in front of you as inducement.'

Ellis eyed him warily. 'What kind of carrot, Mr Baker?'

His smile was smug. 'Your salary would increase, for one thing, in line with the change of title which goes with the job; executive assistant to the company secretary. But...' he paused dramatically, his eyes boring into hers '...the real inducement, Ellis, is the fact that if you work hard enough I see nothing to stop you taking my place when I retire.'

Her breath caught as she gazed at him in disbelief, her eyes like stars. 'Are you serious, Mr Baker?'

'Of course I am. Matt Canning's in full agreement, too, in case that's your next question,' he said, forestalling her. 'So in brief, Ellis, if you want it, the job's yours.'

'When would I start?' she asked eagerly.

Godfrey Baker smiled indulgently. 'I've pressured Matt into letting you go at the end of next week if you say yes. That way you could have a week with Brenda to learn the ropes before you fly solo, so to speak.'

Ellis walked back to her office on air. She sat at her desk, staring into space for a while until Matt Canning strolled through the connecting door.

'You've spoken with Godfrey, I take it?' he remarked.

Ellis jumped up eagerly. 'Yes, Mr Canning, I have. It's a wonderful opportunity. But I realise it will leave you without someone to take my place if I make the changeover so quickly.'

He shook his head indifferently. 'Not at all. Ralph Hayes in personnel says he knows of one or two girls in the building who might do very well. You're free to make the change as soon as you like.'

'Oh. I see,' said Ellis, rebuffed. 'Then in that case, Mr Canning, may I ring Mr Baker and tell him I'll start with him the week after next?'

'Please do. Then, perhaps, we can get on,' he said, already on his way into his office. 'By the way, if I'm obliged to waste time on interviews tomorrow it may mean overtime for you afterwards to make up.'

The remainder of her time as the managing director's secretary flew by on wings. Ellis, secretly nettled that Matt Canning showed no dismay whatsoever at the prospect of her departure, worked herself into the ground to show him what a treasure he was losing. But in her enthusiasm over the new job she decided to abandon her ban on conversation, and admitted to Matt that it had been highly satisfactory to write to the engineering group to request her removal from their short-list.

'I told them that since they'd taken so long I'd found employment elsewhere in the meantime,' she said with satisfaction, reminding Matt she wouldn't need time off for the interview after all.

The grey eyes were ironic as he viewed her jubilant face. 'In other words you told them they could stuff their job.'

'Exactly!' She yawned. 'Goodness, it's late, I must get home.' She paused as she reached the door. 'By the way, Mr Canning, have you decided on my successor yet?'

'Sarah Lewis, the girl from Ralph Hayes's department.'

Ellis nodded. 'Excellent choice, Mr Canning.' Sarah would be over the moon, she thought, amused.

'One thing, though,' said Matt, following her to the door. 'Promise me you'll teach her to make coffee like yours.'

'The least I can do,' she assured him, smiling.

'You know,' he said conversationally, as they went down in the lift together, 'I'd given up hope of ever seeing you smile again. Pretty grim for my ego to know that the prospect of leaving me wrought the miracle.'

'Oh, it's not that,' she assured him blithely. 'It's the joy of not having to drive as far as Gloucester every day that's bucked me up!'

After only a month in her new job Ellis felt like a new woman. She enjoyed working with Godfrey Baker enormously, found the new work stimulating and extending. Yet, much as she relished the new job, she was astonished and rather irritated to find she actually missed working with Matt Canning, something wild horses wouldn't have made her admit. She saw him most days, since he often came in to talk with Godfrey, but Matt rarely spoke to her other than the briefest of greetings. It hurt a little. Which was nonsense, she told herself stringently. Her manner with him had been so hostile after the Clarissa incident that it was a wonder he bothered to say anything to her at all.

Ellis had no time for repining. Her mother and Lydia remonstrated a little when they learned she was going to night classes to brush up on company law. But from the first Godfrey pushed her into taking more and more responsibility, with a view to her eventual succession to his throne, and Ellis entered into it with such a will that Godfrey teased that he might retire a year earlier than anticipated if she continued as she'd begun.

Then one day in late October, when there was a true nip of autumn in the air, Godfrey asked Ellis if she'd do him the honour of dining at his flat the following Saturday.

'Why, I'd love to,' she said, delighted. 'I didn't know you could cook.'

'There are many things you don't know about me, dear girl,' he said loftily. 'But don't expect microscopic scraps in pools of lurid sauce. My *métier* is wholesome, edible food, and plenty of it.'

Ellis found herself looking forward to the evening immensely. Since the débâcle of her evening with Charles she'd hardly gone out at all, other than her weekends at Briar Cottage and her evening classes, or an occasional trip to the cinema or theatre with Vicky

Fisher. It was a sad reflection on her social life, she thought ruefully, when an evening with a man old enough to be her father was cause for excitement. She even went shopping for a new dress in honour of the occasion, and set out that evening arrayed in a brown crêpe slip of a dress, its stark severity highlighted by a dramatic silver chain studded with amber.

Godfrey Baker lived in a large comfortable flat on the outskirts of Pennington Spa. He had a lady who 'did' for him daily, and he was in reach of a restaurant which sent in meals when required, but tonight, he'd promised, the meal would be prepared entirely by his own hands.

Having expected a cosy evening with only Godfrey for company, Ellis felt taken aback when he welcomed her warmly into a room which looked, at first sight, to be packed wall to wall with people. And one head, tawny and unmistakable, loomed tall above the rest.

'Come in, come in, my dear,' said her host jovially. 'I think you know everyone here, Ellis.'

He was right. There were the Maitlands, sincerely pleased to meet her again, the Hennessys, both of whom she liked very much, and, to Ellis's delight, Brenda Harris, enthroned in one of Godfrey's comfortable leather chairs, coaxed away from her retirement fireside to enjoy an evening out. Last, but very far from least, there was Matt Canning, in a suit the colour of Ellis's dress, a gleam in his eye which told her he was well aware of her mixed feelings at the sight of him.

'Brenda, how lovely to see you,' said Ellis, bending to place a kiss on the older woman's cheek.

'You too, dear. Godfrey killing you with work, is he?' said Brenda with a twinkle.

'Of course. But I love it!' Ellis turned at last to Matt with a polite smile. 'Good evening, Mr Canning.'

'Good evening, Ellis. How charming you look. I'm in charge of drinks—what would you like?'

'I indulged in the luxury of a taxi tonight, so a glass of wine, please.'

Almost at once Mrs Maitland pried Ellis away to give her sincere best wishes on the promotion, and it was not until they sat down to the meal that Ellis came into contact with Matt again, when she found herself placed beside him, with Dan Hennessy on her other side.

Over Godfrey's spicy mulligatawny soup Ellis decided it was up to her to make the first conversational move. Since Dan was occupied for the moment with Mrs Maitland, she asked Matt how he was settling in to his new home.

'Very slowly,' he said, shrugging. 'Really I need to take time off to get the place completely straight, but for the moment I just soldier away at weekends.'

'Do you like living out in the country?' she asked politely.

'Very much. But it's nothing new to me. I was born and brought up in a village very like Nether Combe.'

Ellis was surprised. There was little of the country boy about Matt Canning.

'I know your house—by sight, anyway,' she confessed. 'My mother lives fairly near Nether Combe.'

His brows rose. 'Really? Is *that* where you dash off to at weekends?'

'Mostly.' Ellis smiled, then turned to Dan Hennessy to ask him about the progress of his student son, leaving Matt to entertain Brenda Harris, who was plainly quite at home in her surroundings. It was she, Ellis noticed, who helped Godfrey clear away the first course and bring in the next. They were halfway through rare fillet of beef served with roast potatoes and a plain tossed salad before Matt engaged Ellis's attention again.

'Are you happy in the new job?' he asked quietly, under cover of the buzz of conversation round the table. 'I mean really happy?'

'Oh, yes,' Ellis assured him with truth. 'I'm very grateful to Mr Baker for such a wonderful opportunity.'

'Don't attribute him with too much altruism. It was a pretty obvious way to secure a damn good assistant, not to mention the pleasure Godfrey's taking in training you up to replace him one day.'

'Taking my name in vain, Matt?' asked Godfrey slyly, and nodded his full agreement as Matt informed everyone at the table of his prediction as regarded Ellis's future.

Ellis, smiling to cover her embarrassment, felt relieved when Brenda Harris whisked her away to help clear away the plates ready for the next course.

Godfrey's expertise with the stove, he announced, ended with the fillet of beef. To follow he produced an admirably varied cheese board and an enormous bowl of every kind of fresh fruit available. Ellis relaxed again as she enjoyed some perfect grapes, then turned from a conversation with Dan Hennessy to find a neatly peeled nectarine sitting on her plate.

'Olive branch in disguise,' murmured Matt, 'I embarrassed you. I'm sorry.'

'Thank you,' she said, without looking at him, then ate the nectarine to show she accepted his apology.

Ellis had a wonderful time. Godfrey, in his wry, whimsical way, had made no mention of the fact that it was to be something of a party. She'd expected a quiet supper *à deux* with him, which, she assured herself, she'd have enjoyed just as much.

But her pleasure in the evening was, she knew quite well, heightened by the presence of Matt Canning. After dinner he let his long body down on a stool beside the sofa where she was sitting with Brenda Harris, and remained there for most of the evening, other than to help hand round coffee and drinks. It was no big deal, Ellis assured herself. They were the only unattached people in the room in remotely the same age-group. But she was perfectly happy with the arrangement, she found, whatever the reason, and when, much later, she asked Godfrey if she could ring for a taxi to take her home, she thanked Matt gracefully when he offered to drop her off on his way home.

'I won't drive too fast,' he assured her with a grin, as he installed her in the Lotus. 'I've had very little to drink.'

'I noticed.'

'I'm very law-abiding, I promise. It's always seemed crazy to me to trust to luck that some policeman won't stop the car at random and test one's alcohol level.'

'I agree. That's why I came by taxi tonight. For once I rather fancied a glass of wine or two. Normally I couldn't care less whether I have a drink or not.'

'What an abstemious, virtuous pair!' he said mockingly.

'I don't think your opinion of my virtue was very high that night at the Chesterton,' said Ellis, diving in at the deep end.

Matt was silent for so long that she began to wish she'd kept quiet. 'I think,' he said slowly as they turned into Sycamore Road, 'that this particular subject merits a minute or two of discussion to clear the air. Then I vote we forget about it for good.' He switched off the engine then turned to her, his face very sober in the light from the street-lamp. 'It really isn't any of my business what you do out of working hours, Ellis, but that night my sole aim, whether you believe it or not, was to rescue you from the threat of being cited in a divorce case.'

Ellis nodded gravely. 'Yes. I know.'

'My rescue bid was foiled, anyway, wasn't it?' he asked mockingly. 'You blurted out the truth to Clarissa after all, despite my efforts.'

'Yes. But I'm not sorry.' She smiled rather crookedly. 'She would have found out anyway, wouldn't she?'

'The mood she was in, I'm sure you're right.'

Ellis looked at him questioningly. 'Frankly, I'm rather puzzled. I thought people had uncontested divorces these days.'

'Not if one of the parties is unwilling.' Matt eyed her warily. 'And despite all his peccadilloes Charles *is* unwilling, Ellis. Clarissa's the one with the money.'

'Oh. I see.'

'Now, I suppose,' he said heavily, 'I'm in your black books again.'

'Not at all.' Ellis hesitated, reluctant to have the evening end on such a down note. Quickly, before she thought better of the impulse, she said, 'Thank you for bringing me home. Since I can't offer you a drink, would you care for some coffee?'

There was a pause. Matt turned to look at her, as though trying to read her mind. 'Would you like me to come in?'

'I wouldn't have asked you otherwise.'

'Then thank you. I'd like to very much.'

Ellis had left the lights on in her flat. Not of a nervous disposition, she nevertheless considered it only sensible to give her home the appearance of being inhabited when she was out at night. She ushered Matt into her cosy little living-room and invited him to sit down while she made coffee.

Matt grinned. 'I hope it's your usual brew, Ellis. Sarah's a good girl, but her coffee doesn't come up to your standard.'

'I'm sure her work does, which is all that matters, surely!'

Ellis took off her coat and went off to the kitchen, feeling rather pleased with life as she ground coffee beans and boiled water. When she returned with a tray Matt was sprawled on her sofa, leafing through one of her law books, looking very much at home.

He sprang up to take the tray from her. 'It doesn't quite, you know.'

Ellis looked blank. 'What doesn't quite?'

'Sarah's work. She's very good, but not in the same class as you.'

Ellis shrugged. 'You said you didn't need someone like me.'

'For a while I had cause to regret that statement bitterly!' He sipped with relish. 'Particularly while trying to acquire a taste for Sarah's coffee.'

'It can't be that bad! Besides,' added Ellis, taking the chair opposite, 'you should count your blessings. Some places make do with coffee-machines.'

Matt shuddered. 'Over my dead body. Machines do some things better than humans, but coffee's not one of them.' He held out his cup for more, then sat back, looking at her very intently.

'Something wrong?' asked Ellis after a while.

'I'd like to ask you a question. But I can't summon up the nerve to do it.'

Ellis stared. A man more sure of himself than Matt Canning would be hard to find. 'Ask away. I promise not to throw my coffee at you.'

He looked at her very soberly. 'I know I said we should drop the subject, Ellis, but when Longman asked you to work for him at CCS weren't you tempted to say yes?'

'No,' she said curtly. 'I wasn't. But that's not really what you're asking, is it? You're curious to know whether I still cherish any tender feelings for Charles.'

Matt's eyes narrowed to a bright, assessing gleam. 'Yes. You're right. I've never been able to understand what a bright, intelligent girl like you saw in someone like Longman.'

'I don't suppose you do,' she said stiffly.

'Hankering after a married man is a mug's game for a girl like you, in any case. But when the object of it is a lightweight like Charles it's bloody insanity!' he said harshly.

Ellis stared, taken aback by his vehemence.

'Sorry,' he said harshly. 'But something about Longman gets my goat.'

'Why? You're the success. He, I suppose, is the failure. Why *does* he irritate you so much?'

Matt shrugged, looking bitter. 'For reasons which do me no credit, I'm afraid. I object to the fact that his preferment in the organisation owed more to the chairman of the board's friendship at school with Longman's father than to Longman's capability. The school in question, needless to say, was the one Charles graced with his presence in turn.'

Ellis frowned. 'Are you sure? I knew Charles was an Old Etonian, of course. He used to talk about his schooldays a lot. I got the impression he loved his time at Eton so much that everything in his life since has been something of an anticlimax.'

Matt's eyes took on a sardonic gleam. 'Oh, it's true, right enough. Whereas I, my dear Miss Worth, clawed my way to the top with no help at all other than brains, ambition and hard work—plus that certain something known as the cutting edge.'

'You've got that all right!' she said promptly, then bit her lip.

He grinned. 'No need to pull your punches. We're colleagues now, remember.'

She made a face. 'Of a sort. I'm still way out of your league.'

He leapt to his feet, taking her hands to pull her up with him, his eyes glittering with such startling ferocity that she quailed. 'For Pete's sake stop selling yourself short, Ellis. Your years in Longman's shadow are over. The butterfly's out of the chrysalis. Now you're free to spread your wings and develop your true potential. Have confidence in your own ability.'

Ellis lifted her chin. 'But I do. I've no doubts on that score. Once I've got a few years' experience behind me I promise you I'll be as good a company secretary as Godfrey.'

'Absolutely right.' His hands tightened on hers. 'So, are you now over all that nonsense about Longman for good?'

Ellis stiffened, and pulled her hands away. 'It was never nonsense to me! And frankly, I don't see that my personal feelings are anything to do with you.'

'Don't be so hostile, woman! Of course they are.' He raked a hand through his hair, looking exasperated. 'I know you don't work for me any more but I don't see why friendship between us is beyond the bounds of possibility.' He eyed her narrowly. 'Or do you just plain dislike me?'

Ellis, taken by surprise, had to admit she did not. 'Otherwise,' she added with dignity, 'I would hardly have asked you up here tonight.'

'Good. Then I suggest that in future we forget Longman and Clarissa and just proceed on the premise that we're two people with a lot in common professionally, who just might find they have something in common socially too, if granted the opportunity to find out.' He smiled encouragingly. 'Now if you'd like to sit down again, I'll do the same.'

She eyed him warily as she resumed her chair. There was one question she just had to ask, offend or please. 'If we are to be friends there's something I need to know.'

'Ask anything you like.'

'You may *not* like it—that's the trouble.' She looked away. 'The Colcraft grapevine has been buzzing about your move into the Old Rectory—everyone's convinced it means you're getting married soon.'

Matt chuckled, amused, and, she fancied, relieved, as he informed her he intended to inhabit his new home alone for the foreseeable future. 'I did, I confess,' he went on, 'share a home with a lady for a fairly lengthy period several years ago, both during and after my time in college. That was Laura, Clarissa's friend. But in time our paths diverged in the natural way of things, and since then I've been too bloody busy to have much time for the opposite sex on a regular basis—other than the occasional fling,' he added grinning. 'I can't deny the usual male weaknesses, Miss Worth.'

Ellis glared. 'I wasn't asking about those. It's none of my business. I wouldn't have asked anything at all,' she added, 'but after Charles I'm touchy on the subject of married men—even half-promised ones.'

Matt shook his head. 'But surely a woman with your looks must know plenty of eligible men!'

'At one time I did.' She smiled rather ruefully as she told him she'd even got as far as agreeing to marry one of them. Michael had been one of the bright young marketing stars at Colcraft, clever and very ambitious.

'What went wrong?'

'My ambition got in the way. Mike was all for my working for a while after we married. But he just couldn't see why I needed to bother with higher qualifications, when my destiny was marriage and babies and turning myself into the perfect executive wife. When he made a career move to London he gave me an ultimatum.' Her eyes glittered coldly. 'He forced me to choose between him and my ambitions. So I did.'

'Have you ever regretted it?'

'Of course—often. I'm only human.' She jumped up restlessly. 'Let's have some more coffee.'

Matt agreed with flattering promptness, and, when Ellis returned with the coffee-pot, followed her lead when she introduced a less emotive topic of conversation. An hour passed before either of them noticed. It was gone two before Matt looked at his watch and shot to his feet.

'Good grief, Ellis, I had no idea it was so late. I'm sorry.'

'It doesn't matter,' she assured him, feeling for the shoes she'd kicked off at some stage before curling up in her chair. 'Sunday tomorrow. I can sleep in.'

He smiled at her warmly. 'Thank you for the coffee, Ellis, *and* the conversation. I've enjoyed this evening very much, both at Godfrey's place, and, if I'm honest, even more here with you.'

'That's very nice of you.' Ellis smiled back rather sleepily. 'I've enjoyed it too.'

He looked down at her steadily for a moment. 'As a preliminary move towards this new friendship of ours, would you care to lunch with me tomorrow—take a look round my new house?'

Ellis shook her head. 'Sorry.'

His face hardened. 'I see.'

'No, you don't. I'm having lunch with my mother.' She hesitated. 'I could ask her to put back lunch an hour and call by your place for a drink beforehand, if you like.'

Matt thawed instantly. 'Of course I like—I'd forgotten your mother lives in my part of the world.'

'Sunday lunch with Mother and Aunt Lydia is an immovable feast unless I'm very busy, like last Sunday—I'd got a bit behind with my homework. I wouldn't dare back out again this week.'

'No, of course not. Drop by the Old Rectory about twelve, then.' He bent towards her involuntarily, then straightened, a wry smile in his eyes which told her without words that he intended treading very carefully. 'Goodnight. Sleep well.'

CHAPTER SEVEN

ELLIS slept much too well. The morning was half over by the time she tumbled out of bed to ring her mother, asking if lunch could be held back for an hour or so.

'Of course, darling. We can have it any time. Lydia is concocting a rather daring casserole for a change—I'm sure it will hang about as long as you want.' Polly Worth chuckled. 'Slept late after your dinner party?'

When Ellis explained she was making a detour for a drink with Matt Canning on the way to Briar Cottage, her mother could hardly wait to get off the phone to give Lydia the news. A few minutes later, when Ellis was dressing, her mother rang back.

'Lydia says why not ask Mr Canning to share the casserole?'

'I can't do that, Mother!'

'Why not?'

'I'm not on those sort of terms with him. Thank Lydia just the same.'

After wearing formal clothes most of the time during the week, Ellis liked to relax in jeans or track-suits at the weekend. She saw no reason to break the habit for a mere drink with Matt Canning, but honoured the occasion just slightly by wearing a new pair of Levi's and the peach cashmere sweater bought to celebrate her change of fortune.

She was, she admitted, in a very good mood after last night. Since beginning her new job she'd missed contact with Matt rather more than expected. Now he seemed keen to be friends she felt a lot happier. She hated being at odds with anyone. Besides, it was no longer true to say she disliked Matt, or resented him—quite the reverse. But there was no sentiment involved either, which she'd found rather a drag in other relationships in the past. She'd been very fond of Michael, but not enough to sublimate her life in his. And there was Charles, of course. But she wasn't going to think of Charles today. For a change. She would concentrate on the thought that friendship with Matt would be no hardship at all, provided they acknowledged the danger of physical contact—and avoided it.

Ellis sang along with the radio as she joined dawdling Sunday traffic on the road out of Pennington, happier than usual at the wheel as she drove along the road to Nether Combe. Rectory Lane, she found, turned off the main road well before the village itself. Ellis proceeded along it with extra caution, nervous of meeting another vehicle along the narrow lane. As she turned in at last on the new tarmac of the Old Rectory drive she could smell the heady green scent of new cut grass. She parked the car a little way from the house just as Matt came sprinting across the lawn, dressed in sweatshirt and oil-stained denims, his flushed, smiling face beaded with perspiration.

'Welcome to my new abode,' he said, opening the car door for her. 'Sorry about the state of me. I've been giving the lawn its last haircut before winter. I've been at it since the crack of dawn, hoping to have it perfect before you got here, but I lost track of time.'

'It looks wonderful,' she assured him, then turned to look at his new home, which was freshly painted white. Regular as a child's drawing, the house had two windows either side of the twin-pillared portico outside the front door, five on the second storey, each of them divided into twelve panes of glass in true Georgian style. 'I like your house,' she said warmly.

'I'm glad. I like it too. The front door's locked. Come round the back.' Matt led her along a flag-stoned path through a door standing half open into a kitchen furnished with a square table and rush-seated chairs. Plants stood on the windowsills and a bright green oil-fired Aga gave out welcoming warmth. 'If I leave you here for five minutes while I take a shower, could you look at the Sunday papers, Ellis? I should have knocked off sooner to clean up in honour of my guest.' He looked her up and down appreciatively. 'You put me to shame.'

Ellis told him she'd be perfectly happy on her own, and he dashed from the room, humming as he took the stairs two at a time to the floor above. Left alone, she found her surroundings far more interesting than the Sunday papers. Matt Canning liked everything in spick-and-span order, that was plain, but his tidy kitchen wore the look of a room in constant use. There were cookbooks on a shelf, a row of lethal-looking kitchen knives, a chopping-block. A heavy cast-iron pot sat simmering on the Aga, the fragrance from it reminding Ellis she'd missed breakfast. She smiled as she found a cafetière similar to her own, and ready-ground coffee in a jar beside it. A kettle singing away at the back of the stove was too much temptation. On impulse Ellis drew it over the heat and measured coffee into the pot, hoping Matt wouldn't think she was making herself too much at home.

She turned, rather guiltily, as he came back into the room looking lithe and healthy, the colour fresh in his tanned cheeks, his hair dark with water from the shower. He wore a heavy oatmeal cable sweater and baggy brown cords, and looked younger and less formidable than the man who ran such a tight ship at Colcraft Holdings.

'I hope you don't mind,' said Ellis. 'I made some coffee. The smell of whatever's in that pot reminded me I hadn't had any breakfast.'

He looked pleased. 'Why would I mind? Make yourself at home. But I strongly disapprove of people who skip breakfast. You must have some biscuits as well before I bore you to death by showing you through all my empty rooms.'

They sat at the big table, talking at ease with each other as they disposed of the entire contents of the coffee-pot and a packet of oatcakes. The chasm which had opened up between them during the last days spent working together might never have been. Ellis found it hard to believe she'd felt such bitter resentment towards Matt only a couple of months earlier. She'd wondered if it would be hard to go on from where they'd left off the night before, but Matt quite obviously took it for granted this was how things were going to be from now on. And Ellis fell in with him, finding it enormously stimulating to be treated as an intelligent person in her own right, rather than as some kind of extension to another man's personality.

They discovered common interests in music and films, agreed to disagree on some of their literary tastes, and all too soon it was time for Ellis to leave.

'But you haven't had a drink yet—or seen the rest of the house!' protested Matt.

Ellis smiled, surprised to find she was no more eager to go than he was to let her. 'Perhaps some other time.'

'I'll hold you to that!' he said promptly, and held out his hand, then dropped it again, his eyes rueful as he told her without words the effort he was making.

She smiled in silent acknowledgement. 'I've already postponed lunch an hour at Briar Cottage. Can't have my mother and aunt fainting from malnutrition—they were all for having me invite you to lunch as well, by the way, but I refused on your behalf.'

'Why?' asked Matt.

Ellis stared at him in surprise. 'I didn't dream you'd want to.'

He shook his head mockingly. 'Didn't you, now? But then, you don't know me very well. Yet.'

Ellis made no comment. She smiled and thanked him for the coffee. 'I *must* go, but I love your house.'

'You haven't seen any of it yet.'

'The kitchen alone predisposes me towards the rest of it!'

Matt refused to let her go without a lightning tour of the wild, neglected garden at the back of the house, where apple trees fought for existence among weeds he was clearing bit by bit in what time he had to spare.

'Lord knows when I'll get to that jungle behind the trees. On the blurb it was described in estate-agent whimsy as a shrubbery.' Matt eyed the impenetrable tangle with gloom. 'Sleeping Beauty could be in there somewhere for all I know.'

'Why don't you get some help?' suggested Ellis practically. 'In a place like Nether Combe there's usually a little man somewhere willing to put in a few hours.'

Matt liked the idea. 'Where would I find out?'

'In the pub, of course!' Ellis laughed as she got in the car, telling him all he had to do was go through the churchyard, turn left and follow his nose to the Green Man.

'I'll go now,' he said with alacrity, then bent to look in at the car window. 'Sure you won't come with me?'

She shook her head. 'Duty calls—and not just duty. I love my guardian angels very much.'

'I'd very much like to meet them.'

Ellis looked at him in surprise. 'Would you?'

'Yes, I would.' He grinned. 'I'd be coming with you right now if you hadn't turned down my invitation out of hand.'

She shook her head, smiling. 'It's no good trying to make me feel guilty. I know perfectly well you've got something delicious simmering on your stove!'

'Ah, but I'll be eating it alone. It won't be the same!'

Ellis waved goodbye from the window of her car, then found she was smiling rather like the Cheshire Cat as she negotiated the perilous bends of Rectory Lane on her way to Briar Cottage.

Life at Colcraft Holdings took on a new zest for Ellis. There was no perceptible change in Matt Canning's attitude towards her as far as the outside world was concerned. For one thing he was away for part of every week on a systematic tour of all the subsidiary companies, which meant she saw relatively little of him during working hours. And when they did meet their exchanges were little different from before to the undiscerning eye. Lack of discernment, however, was not one of Godfrey Baker's shortcomings.

'You two make a good pair,' he commented, after a heated three-cornered discussion on some proposed company policy after work one day. 'Your minds work in the same way, yet you strike sparks off each other now and then. I fancy Matt enjoys sparring with you, Ellis.'

'I like a good argument,' Ellis admitted, getting ready to leave for the day. 'And I know you do, you Machiavelli. You sit there with your long spoon stirring things up like Old Nick himself.'

'Things need stirring up occasionally,' said Godfrey smugly. 'Get home safely the other night?'

Ellis pursed her lips. 'Yes, thank you, Mr Baker.'

He guffawed. 'No good looking prim, my girl. Don't try and gammon me you objected to Matt's escort, because it won't wash.'

'Then I won't!'

Towards the end of the following week Ellis stayed behind after everyone was gone, working late on research into the company pension fund. She lost track of time completely, so absorbed that she came to with a start to find Matt in the doorway, eyeing her accusingly.

'What the hell are you doing?' he demanded.

'I was just finishing these figures for Godfrey. He needs them in the morning.'

'Put them away,' he said very quietly.

Ellis glared. 'Is that an order?'

'No, dammit, it's a request!' He strode towards her, putting an ungentle finger under her chin. 'You've got purple rings round your eyes, woman. You may be in love with your job, but this is damn stupid. Have you any idea what time it is?'

'You're still here,' she pointed out.

He released her and stood back. 'That's different.'

'Ah! Because you're the boss, you mean.'

'Don't be petty. I meant that I don't feel anything like as exhausted as you look. Come on. I'm not budging until you're ready to go.'

'Oh, very well,' she said irritably, and began tidying up. 'Do you go round all the offices, shooing people out if they work late?'

'No.'

'Then why come the despot where I'm concerned?'

'I came to leave a note for Godfrey. It never occurred to me you'd still be here at this hour.' He shrugged. 'Actually I was going to ring you later, but now you're here I can make my request in person.'

Ellis slid her arms into her jacket, eyeing him curiously. 'Is there something you want me to do for you?'

Matt perched himself on the corner of her desk. 'There's an Agatha Christie on at Pennington Rep all this week. I've got two tickets for Saturday night. Will you come with me?'

Ellis eyed him thoughtfully, then pointed out that the local playhouse was a popular haunt with quite a few Colcraft employees. Her presence there with the MD would provide a juicy titbit of gossip in the works cafeteria the following week.

'Would that worry you?'

Ellis shrugged. 'If you don't mind, why should I?'

'It's not breaking any law for two unattached individuals, well over the age of consent, to take a trip to the theatre together!'

'True.' She grinned at him cheekily. 'I'll be the envy of all my female colleagues, you know.'

Matt's eyes narrowed. 'Why?'

She hooted. 'Oh, come on! You're the most eligible bachelor in a twenty-mile radius, according to certain of your lady employees.'

'You're joking!'

'I'm not. There was much gnashing of teeth and wailing when you bought the Old Rectory because they were all, to a woman, convinced you were about to surrender your bachelor status.' Ellis smiled demurely. 'No gnashing on my part, of course.'

Matt's lips twitched. 'Of course. So, since you're the only nubile female in this part of the county still not breathing down my neck—according to you—I shall feel perfectly safe in your company at the theatre on Saturday, won't I?'

'After which *I'll* be the main topic of conversation,' she said, resigned.

'Do you care?'

Ellis thought about for a moment, then shook her head. 'No. Not really. Besides, I can't resist Agatha Christie plays. I never know who's done the deed until they all gather in the library at the end for the showdown—why is it always the library?'

Ellis had a great fondness for the Spa Theatre. Recently restored to its rococo Victorian splendour, it had an excellent repertory company, and every so often boasted star names in a play trying out in the provinces before going into the West End. Saturday night always drew a packed house whatever was playing, and Ellis pushed aside her law books in keen anticipation when it was time to get ready.

Dressed in her brown skirt and oyster jacket, with an outsize sweep of cream wool on top against the cold November night, Ellis was adding a final touch of lipstick when Matt arrived.

'Delightful to look at and punctual as usual!' He frowned as he caught sight of the textbooks scattered everywhere.

'Sorry for the mess,' said Ellis, as she locked up behind them. 'My night class on Thursday convinced me I need to get down to some really solid work.'

'Don't push yourself so hard,' advised Matt. 'All work and no play is a bad thing, remember?'

'Well, it's play tonight, and I'm looking forward to it. I adore that moment when the lights go down.'

'Ditto. And I promise to keep quiet if I guess whodunit.'

'Very prudent—otherwise they'll have an extra murder on their hands!'

As expected they encountered several familiar faces in the circle bar when they went for a drink at the end of the first act, but Ellis refused to let it spoil her evening.

'Do you feel thoroughly compromised?' Matt teased as they settled in their seats again.

'Certainly not. Hush—the butler's found the missing letter!'

They had supper afterwards in a small Italian restaurant where Ellis talked non-stop over her spaghetti carbonara, still marvelling that the murderer had been the last one she'd suspected.

'Heavens, just listen to me rattling on,' she said after a while. 'You haven't got a word in—why are you grinning from ear to ear like that?'

'I was just thinking how good it was to hear you talking your head off after that glacial silence you

inflicted on me a couple of months back!' The corners
of his mouth went down. 'My office felt like a deep
freeze.'

'Good! You deserved it——' She bit her lip. 'Now,
I suppose, you'll sack me for being rude to the managing director!'

'Not if you come to lunch with me tomorrow.'

Ellis stared, taken aback.

'I mean it,' Matt persisted. 'Or are you committed
to lunch with your mother again?'

'No, as it happens. I cried off this week to get down
to some revision.'

'Get up early, put a couple of hours in, then come
to lunch with me. You can get back to your books
later in the day.' He smiled persuasively. 'You'll need
to eat, so why not eat with me? This time you can see
round the rest of the house.'

Ellis very nearly said yes there and then, but an
inner voice advised caution. 'I'll think about it.'

'Couldn't you break the habit of a lifetime and say
yes spontaneously for once?' sighed Matt, signalling
to the waiter.

'No.' Ellis smiled to take the sting out of the negative. 'Not my style. Besides, I'm not intending to think
about it longer than the drive home.'

She was as good as her word. When they reached
the flat she unlocked the door, then asked him if he'd
like some coffee.

'Of course I would,' he said, clearing some textbooks from the sofa so that he could sit down. 'I
would also like a reply to my invitation to lunch—
preferably in the affirmative.'

'All right,' she agreed blithely, and slung her shawl over the back of the chair, then went off to make coffee.

'Well?' Matt demanded impatiently, when Ellis returned with a tray.

'Well what?' she said innocently.

'I'm waiting for your answer, blast it!' he exploded.

'I've given it.'

'When?'

'Just now. I said all right.'

Matt took the cup she handed him, his smile ironic. 'Pardon my mistake. Your enthusiasm misled me.'

'Ah! Other women, I assume, smother you with gratitude when you offer to feed them.'

'Not exactly. But they usually give me a straight yes or no.'

Ellis hooted. 'Tell the truth. You mean they always say yes!'

He smirked outrageously. 'Of course.'

She shook her head at him, her eyes bright with amusement as she took his cup and placed it, very pointedly, on the tray.

Matt sighed. 'I'm going, I'm going. Otherwise you'll be late starting on those blasted books in the morning and ring to cancel lunch.'

'Not at all. Once I've said yes I keep to it!'

Light flared in his eyes. 'Then in that case——' He leapt to his feet and caught her in his arms all in one movement, holding her fast as she tried to escape.

Ellis glared up at him, her resentment escalating as she found she didn't want to escape. 'Let me go, Matt. I agreed to a trip to the theatre, not—not——'

'Not what?' he asked, the look of calm reason in his eyes belying the rapidity of his heartbeat. Ellis could feel it, hammering, through the layers of their clothes; felt her own heart race in response.

'All I ask,' he said, his voice a fraction uneven, 'is a goodnight kiss. One kiss between friends. Is that so unreasonable?'

But even as he spoke the cool reason in his eyes was gone, giving way to a heat which intensified as the encroaching dark rims widened, blotting out the cool grey iris, and Ellis gazed, ensnared, unable to look away.

'In theory, no,' she said unsteadily. 'But in practice it doesn't seem to work like that.'

'One kiss,' he said inexorably, and bent his head until his lips met hers. The merest touch of mouth on mouth ignited a response in each other so immediate and overwhelming that Ellis abandoned all pretence of opposition. She yielded, dazed, to the pressure of his arms, her body curving pliantly into his, as the kiss went on and on until neither could breathe.

Matt raised his head slowly at last, his eyes glittering darkly in his set face. He crushed her to him for a moment then released her so abruptly that she stumbled, and he put out a hand to steady her.

'Are you all right?'

She blinked owlishly. 'Not—not quite. I feel as if I've been dropped from a great height.'

'I kept scrupulously to the one kiss,' he pointed out.

'Is that all it was?'

'Definitely. I kept to the letter of the agreement.'

'*You* agreed. I didn't.'

'But you hesitated, Ellis. Remember what happens to she who hesitates!' Matt's eyes narrowed suddenly. 'Only I'm probably the one who's lost. I suppose you've changed your mind now about tomorrow.'

Ellis shook her head. 'No. I said I'd come, and I will.' She eyed him significantly. 'But on one condition, Matt.'

'I know, I know. No kisses.' He shrugged philosophically. 'Whatever you say.' He thrust back a lock of bright hair, suddenly in deadly earnest. 'Ellis, the idea of friendship between us pleases me a great deal. But at the risk of ruining it before it's even begun I'd better make it clear right now that I can't promise to rule out physical demonstrations between us. You're a very good-looking lady, and I'm a normal sort of male. And over and above all that you must admit that something quite extraordinary happens every time we kiss.' Matt smiled at her wryly, then held a hand up like someone making a declaration in court. 'But I solemnly swear I'll never ask anything more of you that you're not willing to give of your own free will.'

CHAPTER EIGHT

WHEN Ellis arrived at the Old Rectory in Nether Combe the next day she found Matt waiting for her in the garden, wearing jeans and a sweater and an open-necked shirt. He looked as if he'd spent all morning out in the pale winter sunshine which struck fiery sparks from his hair as he bent to open her car door.

'So you actually made it,' was his greeting.

'Weren't you expecting me to?'

'After my parting speech last night I thought you might chicken out.' He smiled, eyeing her green cords and canary-yellow sweater with approval. 'You look gorgeous.'

'Thank you, kind sir,' she said demurely. 'I'm as susceptible to compliments as any other woman.'

'You're nothing like any other woman I've known,' he said, ushering her before him into the house. 'In my opinion you, Miss Ellis Worth, are one of a kind.'

'Everyone is,' she said tartly, then stopped short in the large, square hall, her eyes shining as she took in the sheen of newly stripped wood floors, the ex-quisite, faded colours of the rug Matt told her he'd run to earth in a place which dealt in second-hand Persian carpets.

The drawing-room was almost as uncluttered as the hall. The carpet here was fringed and vast, woven with faded tints of ivory and black and russet. Matt con-fessed he'd chosen the colour-scheme around it, had

129

the walls painted pale terracotta, and the tall windows hung with heavy ivory moire caught back with thick ropes of russet silk. Apart from two large, studded leather chairs either side of the fireplace a long, chintz-covered sofa was the only piece of furniture in the room.

'Not much to show yet, I'm afraid,' said Matt. 'I got Marston's in Pennington to do the curtains once the painting was done, but I've been a bit short on time to make any more progress.'

'It's a lovely room,' said Ellis with sincerity. 'That carved fireplace is a gem. Will you burn logs in it?'

'You bet I will. After all my hacking and chopping in the garden I've got enough wood for years! Come and see the rest of the house.'

Matt's book-lined study was relatively fully furnished, with a leather-topped table littered with paperwork and a functional modern desk for his computer. Ellis made a face at the familiar machinery, took a quick peep at the vast, unfurnished dining-room, then made a bee-line for the warmth of the kitchen.

'I'll show you the upper floor presently,' said Matt. He bent to inspect something in the Aga, releasing mouth-watering scents of rosemary and garlic. 'I'd better keep an eye on lunch for the time being.' He straightened, grinning. 'I'm no expert cook, I should warn you.'

'Neither am I,' Ellis assured him. 'Can I help?'

'In a minute, if you like. But for the moment I fancy a drink. What will you have?'

'If you're opening wine for lunch I'll have a glass of that, please.'

They sat at the kitchen table with their d
cussing a controversial article in the Sund
while saucepans bubbled on the stove, and a big clock
ticked companionably on the wall. Ellis, a little wary
at first after the charged incident of the night before,
found herself relaxing, attuned to the feeling of grace
in the very air of the house.

'What are you thinking?' asked Matt softly.

'I was just soaking up the atmosphere.'

He nodded. 'It's a very seductive house.'

She smiled. 'Seductive?'

'Yes. Originally I had my mind set on somewhere
modern, ready-fitted, automatic everything, preferably right in the centre of Pennington. But the
moment I set foot in this place I was lost.'

Ellis nodded. 'I know what you mean—but it's a
bit on the large side. You could put my entire flat in
this room with a push.'

'When I said I was going to live here alone the estate
agent had obvious doubts about my sanity!' Matt
jumped to his feet to inspect the contents of the
saucepans.

'It's a lot of house for one person.'

He grinned. 'Perhaps I should change the name to
"Canning's Folly"—I hope you like lamb, by the
way.'

Ellis assured him she did, and helped him lay the
kitchen table, then put the vegetables in the warming-
oven while Matt took the first course from the
refrigerator.

'Smoked salmon—unimaginative, but easy,' he
said, pulling out a chair for Ellis. 'Let's drink a toast.'
He raised his glass of wine to her. 'To friendship—
and to more occasions like this.'

Ellis clinked glasses with him, smiling. 'I'll drink to that.'

As they enjoyed the simple, delicious meal they turned inevitably to talk of Colcraft and Matt's plans for the future, the conversation flowing so freely between them that they lingered at the table, engrossed, long after the meal was over and the coffee-pot empty. At last Ellis jumped to her feet briskly, turning a deaf ear to Matt's pleas to leave the washing-up for later. When it was all done she asked for a closer look at the garden, which had lain neglected for years behind its sequestering hedges of hawthorn and privet.

'These borders could do with weeding,' she said with disapproval, as they strolled along the gravel paths.

'Have a heart! I'm still at the strimmer and chainsaw stage. I haven't got to grips with trowel and fork yet.'

'Got any gloves?' she demanded.

He looked taken aback. 'Why?'

'I quite like a spot of weeding.'

'You'll spoil your clothes.'

'My clothes will wash. Just hand me the tools, Mr Canning, and I'll get on with the job.'

Minutes later both of them were hard at work on their knees, a wheelbarrow at hand for the debris as they battled with weeds left to flourish unchallenged for far too long.

'Be careful,' warned Ellis. 'There may be crocuses and snowdrops under here, not to mention daffodil bulbs.'

'Yes, ma'am.'

They worked together until the light faded to the point where Matt declared he couldn't tell weeds from plants.

'Time we called it a day,' he said firmly.

Ellis jumped back to her feet, brushing her hair back with her sleeve, as she looked at her watch. 'Good heavens, is that the time? I must go.'

'Why?'

'It's late.'

Matt smiled persuasively as he opened the door. 'Is there any reason for you to rush home?'

'I'm supposed to be boning up on company law, remember!'

In the sudden, bright light of the kitchen he looked at her sternly. 'An hour or two off won't do you any harm, surely! Dammit, Ellis, why do I have to fight for every little concession? Do you have some hang-up about saying yes?'

'No,' she said, then laughed as he rolled his eyes heavenwards. 'But I came for lunch, not the entire day, Matt.'

'Most of which you spent in weeding the garden.' He put out a dirty finger to touch her cheek. 'I insist you stay for some tea. Go and wash your face; you've smeared it with mud.'

She eyed him mutinously for a moment, then shrugged. 'All right. I would like some tea. But after that it's back to my books.'

Matt directed her upstairs to the guest bathroom on the floor above. 'Take a look round while you're at it. I'll have tea waiting by the time you come down.'

Ellis washed quickly in a bathroom resplendent with claw-footed bath and brass taps, then made a lightning tour of the bedrooms. There were four of them, all large, light and airy, but empty except for Matt's, which had the same spare, uncluttered look as the rest of the house. Deciding his penchant for earth tones needed spicing up with a splash of colour somewhere, she went back down to Matt to find he'd set a tea tray with thin fluted cups and a silver teapot, also a tempting iced cake decorated with walnuts.

'Now don't tell me you made that while I was up-stairs!' she said, laughing.

Matt sprang up to hold her chair, looking smug. 'I've found a quite wonderful lady by the name of Mrs Pope who's promised to "do" for me three times a week. She insisted on baking the cake when I said I hoped to have a guest today.'

Ellis raised her eyebrows. 'How did you know I'd come?'

'I didn't. I said "hoped".' He shrugged. 'If you'd refused—again—I'd have shared the cake with Mrs Pope and Sam Draper.'

'Who's Sam Draper?'

'He's the "little man" I heard of at the Green Man, as you thought I might. He's agreed to the same three mornings as Mrs Pope—he must know she bakes cakes like this! Try some.'

Ellis accepted a slice of cake, agreeing after only a mouthful that Matt had been extremely lucky to find Mrs Pope. 'Did you foresee all this extra expense when you took on the house?' she asked curiously.

'Of course I did.' He smiled mockingly. 'You know me better than that, Ellis! I calculated to a penny how much it would set me back, including the fortune spent on bathroom and kitchen fittings.'

'Are you sorry?'

He grinned. 'No, I'm not. I'm so besotted with the damn house I'll buy it anything it wants.'

As Matt went on discussing the improvements he meant to make Ellis realised she not only felt a little tired after her exertions, but dangerously comfortable in the warmth of the kitchen. Rain lashed suddenly against the windows, and she jumped to her feet, suddenly brisk. 'I must go—and this time I mean it. It's disgracefully late for a lunch guest.'

'Lunch guests rarely spend the post-prandial hours digging the garden!' Matt took her hand. 'My thanks, Ellis. For coming, and the gardening, and generally making my day the most pleasant I've spent in a long time.'

'I've enjoyed it too.'

Matt's fingers tightened on hers involuntarily. 'Ellis . . .' He hesitated, looking down into her eyes, then gave a despairing shrug and took her in his arms. 'I know, I know—you said no kisses. But having you here alone like this is murder on my self-restraint— why aren't you fighting to get away?' he added, surprised.

Ellis looked up at him steadily. 'You made it clear last night you'd expect a kiss or two.'

'Can I expect one right now?'

'What do I have to do?' she asked crossly. 'Send you a memo?'

Matt hauled her up on tiptoe, almost rough with her as his mouth fired her into instant response, and Ellis locked her arms about his neck to keep her balance. She returned his kisses with a lack of inhibition which almost put paid to Matt's restraint altogether, and he tore his mouth away, breathing hard. 'There's one snag about this!'

Ellis leaned back against his clasped arms until she was standing on her own two feet again. 'What's that?'

'This—this reaction we trigger off between us. I find I can't stop thinking about it.' His eyes glittered darkly. 'Before I met you I kept women in separate compartments labelled "work" or "play". Never mixed. But you're different. *Very* different. One moment we can be discussing company policy, or the latest government bill—and the next all I can think of is how much I want you in my arms.'

'That really is a snag,' she admitted breathlessly.

'You know exactly what I'm getting at, Ellis.' He touched the tip of her nose with his finger. 'We're two mature adults. We both know what I'll want—what I'll damn well *crave* if we play with fire. I pride myself on a reasonable amount of self-control, but dammit, Ellis, I'm only human.'

'So what's the answer?' asked Ellis, as he ran with her to the car, shielding her under a large golf umbrella. 'Is it best to call it quits before things get out of hand?'

Matt stopped in his tracks. 'Is that what *you* want?' he demanded.

'Do you?' she countered.

'You know damn well I don't!'

'Then the answer's simple. Take away the matches and you can't start a fire—in other words a fine friendship, but no kisses.'

His mouth twisted. 'Shouldn't that be "romance"?'

Ellis shook her head firmly and got in the car, winding down her window to smile up at him. 'No fear. I've tried romance—and got my fingers burnt. But I'm willing to settle for friendship, if you want.'

With a casual little wave she drove away down the drive, flashing her lights in salute as she turned into the lane.

Ellis's evening with Matt at the theatre did not, as expected, go unmarked. At lunch the following Monday she spiked Vicky and Sarah's guns by giving them a short résumé of the evening before they'd plucked up the courage to ask her about it.

'He had two tickets for the play, so he asked me to go with him,' said Ellis, going on with her lunch matter-of-factly. 'Afterwards we went to the Napoli for spaghetti carbonara, and after that he took me home. Any questions?'

Both girls were obviously bursting with questions, but a certain light in Ellis's eye decided them against asking any. However, since Matt took her out to a meal again a few days later, and to a concert at the weekend, it was useless for Ellis to pretend that her relationship with him as as casual as she'd implied.

'But what do you *talk* about?' asked Vicky one day. 'He terrifies me if he even asks me to leave a message for Mr Hennessy.'

Sarah looked wistful. 'He doesn't terrify *me*. Actually he's surprisingly nice to work for, but ...'

'But what?' asked Ellis .

'Well, he's so very impersonal somehow. As though I don't have a gender at all. To him I'm just a satisfactory employee.'

Since Sarah was a very attractive blonde Ellis was rather surprised by this interesting piece of information—and more than a little pleased that Matt kept his secretary in a compartment labelled 'work'.

* * *

As end of term loomed nearer Ellis restricted outings with Matt to Saturday evenings only, with her Sunday lunch at Briar Cottage the only other distraction from her law studies.

'My lecturer is setting an end-of-term exam,' she told Matt one night at the Trout Inn. 'I'm determined to do well.'

Matt eyed her wryly across the small candlelit table. 'Your career means a great deal to you, doesn't it?'

'I'm one of the lucky ones—I enjoy my work. I'd hate to do a job just for the money.'

'Don't you ever think about marriage, Ellis?'

'I'm not against the idea. I'm a normal sort of female really. I'd like a family, just like anyone else.' Ellis smiled at him. 'The problem is, Matt, I'm greedy. I'd want it all—home, children *and* career.'

'Wouldn't a husband have to feature in there somewhere too?' he asked drily.

'Ah, but not every man wants a wife dedicated to a career. Michael certainly didn't,' she added soberly, then changed the subject. 'Tell me, what's this I hear about a different kind of Christmas party this year?'

Matt grinned. 'Sarah's been talking, I gather.'

'Only to me!' said Ellis quickly.

'No need to defend her. It's nothing confidential— the invitations will be out next week.'

'It's something new to invite the whole workforce at Colcraft to a Christmas Ball.' Ellis's eyes sparkled. 'I bet some of the old guard will be miffed. Before you came only management had the privilege of a dinner-dance. *Hoi polloi* had a sort of social evening in the cafeteria.'

Matt informed her it was good for work relations. 'I've invited people from the various subsidiaries as well,' he added casually.

'Including the Longmans,' said Ellis, resigned.

'I could hardly leave them out!'

'I suppose not.'

'And I want you there,' he said, holding her eyes very deliberately, 'whether the Longmans turn up or not.'

'Of course,' she said airily. 'I wouldn't miss it for the world.'

On the journey back Ellis became preoccupied, as usual, with the question of whether to ask Matt up to her flat for coffee. He'd kept scrupulously to her 'no kisses' decree ever since the protracted lunch at the Old Rectory—so scrupulously that she was beginning to regret she'd ever mentioned it. At the same time he'd made it very clear that the only way he could keep to it was to avoid being alone with her in private, which ruled out any time spent together in her flat or at the Old Rectory, something she regretted more and more as she got to know Matt better.

But when the Lotus drew up in Sycamore Road Matt took the wind out of Ellis's sails by asking her if he could come in for a while for once. 'Don't worry,' he added coolly, 'I won't break any rules. I want to discuss something with you in private.'

Ellis felt intrigued as she ushered him into her flat. 'Coffee?' she asked.

'No, thanks, Ellis.' Matt motioned her to a chair. 'Just sit down for a moment and listen, if you would.'

Apprehensive now, Ellis took off her coat and sat, eyeing him warily. 'Something wrong?' she asked.

'No. At least not yet,' he said elliptically, and sat down on the edge of her sofa, leaning forward slightly with his hands linked between his knees. 'I'd like to enlarge on the subject we discussed over dinner.'

'The dance? Do you want me to help organise——?'

'No! It's nothing to do with the bloody dance!' he snapped, then checked himself. 'Sorry, Ellis. The particular discussion I'm referring to is the one about your career.'

Ellis tensed. 'Are you dissatisfied with my progress, then?'

'Of course not, woman! You're doing brilliantly—and you know it.' He thought for a moment. 'Look, Ellis, I think the best way to explain what I mean is to tell you a little story.'

'Good. I love stories.'

Matt looked sceptical. 'I doubt if you'll enjoy this one. It's not a very appetising little tale. It starts when I was about sixteen or so. My father lectured in economics at a polytechnic. While I was still at school he left my mother for one of his students, a girl not much older than me.'

Ellis sat very still, hardly daring to breathe as Matt went on to talk about the way his father had tried to placate him before he left, giving explanations that shamed and embarrassed the young Matt. His mother, too shattered to appreciate the depth of her son's misery, had fled to her parents in Norwich, after paying for Matt to board at the school he'd previously attended as a day boy. Isolated, grieving, his schoolwork deteriorating, the bottom had dropped out of Matt's world entirely when his mother quickly found consolation with an American businessman on a nostalgia trip to the airfields he'd flown from during World War Two.

'Cal consoled her so successfully that she went off to the States to marry him as soon as her divorce from my father came through. I was left to a peripatetic existence of school, grandparents, odd weeks with my father and his new family, plus the occasional flight across the Atlantic to Boston to stay with Mr and Mrs Calvert Jackson.'

'Do you still see them?' asked Ellis quietly.

'My mother died a couple of years ago, but I keep in touch with Cal. And very occasionally I make the trip down to Devon to see my father and Sheila.'

'Do you still feel bitter towards your father?'

'Not any more. I was once. I blamed my parents for every single thing that went wrong in my life. When I was in school I had my sights set on Oxford. Owing to the upheaval I didn't do well enough to get in and had to settle for a lesser hall of learning, where I worked hard, played hard and emerged with a good degree and a burning ambition to set the world on fire.' He smiled at her wryly. 'Thanks to Cal Jackson I was lucky enough to follow it up with a stint at Harvard Business School. Then when I came back to this country I began working my way up the ladder, learning the dog-eat-dog skills of my calling on every rung from the bottom to the top.'

'Where you arrived pretty quickly!' Ellis smiled warmly. 'Your father must be very proud of you.'

'If he is he never says so.' Matt leaned forward to take her hands, his eyes bitter. 'But the point of all this discourse, Ellis, is that between them my esteemed parents taught me a very valuable lesson. Namely that love, or what passes for it, is not an

emotion to trust. Both of them were wildly in love
with each other when they married. When I was a
child they were like a pair of young lovers together—
it was embarrassing. Then hey presto, all that went
out the window when my father fell in love just as
madly with the nubile Sheila, and left my mother flat.
I suppose, looking at it with hindsight, I might have
coped better at the time if my mother hadn't been so
quick to find consolation with Cal. That was the final
straw.'

'You must have been devastated,' said Ellis with
sympathy.

'I was, but in a way the experience was valuable.'
His smile was bleak. 'It taught me that relationships
with women are best compartmented, as I said before.
Some for play, some for work, with no nonsense about
love to fog up the issue.' Matt jumped up suddenly,
as though he could no longer sit still, pulling her up
with him.

Ellis eyed him with misgiving, half of her com-
passionate towards the boy Matt had been, the other
half chilled by the man he'd become. The man with
no place in his life for love.

'I see,' she said dully, and tried to free her wrists,
but Matt held her fast. She gazed at him in suspicion
as he began to talk in a lucid, reasoning way familiar
to her from a score of meetings at Colcraft.

'Until I met you, Ellis, I never realised what a gap
there was in my life. My work has always been enough.
And there was always some attractive woman on the
periphery of my life whenever I felt the urge to play.'
He drew her closer. 'With you it's different. You just
won't stay in a neatly labelled compartment. You're
desirable, but you're clever, ambitious as well as

beautiful. And, for some reason I fail to understand, you don't seem to have a man in your life—except me,' he added with a crooked smile.

Ellis raised her chin. 'So what label are you going to stick on me?'

'That depends on you.'

'I don't understand.'

'Then let me explain. You see, Ellis Worth, I think you and I have a lot in common. I admire your capacity for hard work, the way your mind functions, your determination to climb to the top of the tree. But I also like your warmth, the way your eyes flash green when you're angry, the way you nibble at that sensuous lower lip of yours when you're concentrating, the intelligence which sets your face apart from mere good looks—and,' he added very softly, 'the body which goes with the face.'

'Matt——' she began, but he laid a peremptory finger on her lips.

'Come and sit down, Ellis. I've got a proposition to put to you.'

Proposition? Ellis tensed as he drew her down beside him on the sofa.

'Since I moved into the Old Rectory I've come to realise just what it is my life lacks,' he began. 'Every time I think of buying something for the house I hold back, wanting you with me to help me choose. But I've known all along that the house doesn't just need *things* to go in it, Ellis. It needs a woman. And so do I.'

Ellis leapt to her feet at the last, but Matt caught her easily, silencing her protest with a kiss meant to make nonsense of her opposition. It was a long time before he lifted his head to stare into her eyes, the cool grey of his own transformed to the dark glitter she knew spelt trouble.

'I think you'd better let me go,' she said gruffly, trying to free herself.

'I have no intention of letting you go,' he said, in a conversational tone at odds with the heat in his eyes. 'Is it so impossible to envisage living with me at the Old Rectory? I hope not, because I warn you now I'll never give up until you say yes.'

Ellis wrenched herself free, then backed away, hugging her arms across her chest as she shook her head violently. 'You can't be serious!'

The molten look faded rapidly. 'As it happens, I am,' Matt informed her coldly.

'I don't think you can have thought it through,' she said, conscious of an illogical and totally unexpected feeling of disappointment. She had received propositions before, she reminded herself stringently. The only difference in this case was that the man happened to head the company she worked for. 'In the circumstances it's out of the question.'

Matt stood erect, his face set. The friendly, attentive companion of the evening was gone. In his place stood the managing director of Colcraft, every formidable inch of him displaying offence at her rejection.

'I fail to see why,' he informed her icily. 'We're both unattached adults...' He paused, eyeing her with sudden cold distaste. 'Unless, of course, you're still languishing over Longman.'

Ellis stared blankly. 'What's Charles got to do with it?'

He shrugged. 'I've no idea. Far be it from me to pretend comprehension of the female mind.'

'Only a short time ago you were rhapsodising over mine!' she snapped.

Matt started forward, seizing her by the elbows. 'All right, Ellis. Listen to me. If Charles is the impediment I've got a lot more to offer you than he has.' He shook her slightly. 'I am, as you told me quite recently, a hell of a sight more successful than he is, with a lot more to offer when it comes to helping you with your career. I've even got a house you admire, ready for you to move into and finish decorating in any way you want. I won't insult you by pretending high-flown emotions I've never experienced, but dammit, Ellis, we could have a good life together, including the part of it we'd spend in bed. *That*,' he said with sudden vehemence, 'would be better than anything either of us will ever find with anyone else and you know it!' He relaxed his grip as she winced slightly. 'Besides, Longman's married, remember, and I'm not—a definite advantage on my part.'

'Oh, yes,' agreed Ellis. 'It is. And I'll be frank. If we worked for different organisations I wouldn't hesitate. But since we do it just isn't on. You're the managing director of the company, so I'm the one who'd have to resign. Which means the answer's no. I'll never get another job in the area with prospects like this one, so I really don't have a choice. I'm sorry, but I must put my career first.'

Matt stepped back, his face set. 'I see. You don't pull your punches, do you, Ellis? You told me recently you weren't opposed to the idea of marriage, so I assume that it's the prospect of marriage to me in particular you can't accept.'

Ellis stood like someone turned to stone. Had he really said marriage, or was she imagining it? She stared at him in silence for so long that he began to frown.

'What is it?' he demanded.

'Indulge me,' she said without inflexion. 'Would you repeat the proposition, please?'

'You mean go through all that again——' Matt stopped, stared, then his eyes lit with sudden laughter. 'Ellis? Have we got our lines crossed somewhere?'

She felt a hard lump of ice inside her begin to melt, flooding her veins with a sensation she decided must be relief. 'I don't know,' she said calmly. 'Have we?'

He regarded her in amusement. 'I think there's some confusion about labels. The one I'm offering is "wife", Ellis. In the circumstances you keep harping on I thought it best if we got married before setting up house together!'

CHAPTER NINE

MARRY Matt Canning? Ellis, convinced he'd been asking her merely to move in with him, felt at a complete loss for a moment. At first glance it was an extraordinary idea. Yet was it? She liked him very much. Far more than she'd have thought possible when they first met. Over the months her respect had grown almost daily for his drive and integrity and keen brain, even for that cutting edge of his which made him indisputable leader of the pack. Her gaze was analytical as it moved from his tawny hair and striking, intent eyes to the formidable build of him. Physical attributes like Matt Canning's, combined with his other, more cerebral qualities, she reflected, were very powerful incentives to marriage.

He stood very still under her scrutiny, his eyes inscrutable as he waited for her response.

'I would have thought,' she said at last, 'that your parents' example would have turned you off marriage for life.'

Matt relaxed slightly, moved closer. 'It did. Until I met you. Now I think it would be the best of all worlds for both of us, Ellis. We're both mature, responsible people. We could have a very good life together—perfect partners privately *and* professionally, which is at least fifty per cent more than most married couples.'

'Most couples marry for love,' Ellis pointed out. 'So—purely a hypothetical question, of course—what would happen if later on one or other of us fell madly in love with someone else? It *could* happen, as you know better than most.'

He shrugged. 'Since I have no intention of falling madly in love with anyone in my entire life the guilty party would be you, Ellis.' He waited for a moment, his eyes willing her to answer. 'So. What do you say?'

She hesitated. 'You make it sound so clinical, so cold-blooded.'

For answer he seized her in his arms, holding her in a grip which threatened her ribs as his eyes locked with hers. 'You're wrong, Ellis. My feelings may not be the fairy-story kind, but don't delude yourself there's anything cold-blooded about them!' And to prove his point beyond all possible doubt he picked her up in his arms and sat down with her on the sofa, kissing her in a way which made it crystal-clear that the ban on physical contact was over with a vengeance. Ellis lay lax in surprise for a moment then began to fight involuntarily against the iron restraint.

He relaxed his hold, his mouth softening as he coaxed her lips apart. As his tongue sought the secret places of her mouth she felt her bones dissolve, her body flow into his. She wreathed her arms about his taut neck and felt a jolt of electricity surge through her at the feel of Matt's heart hammering against her breasts, triumphant when his hands shook slightly as he caressed her. His lips left hers to travel down over her throat, his fingers almost clumsy as they undid her shirt and thrust aside the lace beneath. She felt his hair brush her naked skin, arched her spine with a gasp as his mouth closed on a swollen, waiting nipple, her hands clenched convulsively in his hair as he caressed her with fingers and lips and tongue and the subtle anguish of grazing teeth.

Ellis uttered a strangled sound deep in her throat and thrashed her head back and forth. Matt raised his head to look into her wide, incredulous eyes, then pulled away to shrug himself free of his jacket. He tossed it on the floor then crushed her close, finding her mouth again, his hands tracing every curve and contour of her body with mounting urgency. She gave herself up to him without reserve, her hands seeking the muscles of his shoulders through his thin shirt, holding him closer and closer as his caresses sought new territory. She tensed like a bow as his fingers reached the satin smoothness above her stocking, and Matt breathed in sharply, stiffened, then pulled away to sit with his head in his hands as he fought for control.

Ellis lay where she was for a while, stunned, then sat up and began to put herself together with shaking, uncoordinated hands. At last Matt turned to look at her with an air of such undisguised ownership that Ellis felt her face flame and turned hastily away.

'You see?' he said, very quietly, something in his tone warning her his self-control was far from absolute. 'You and I could have it all, Ellis. A partnership complete in every way.'

In every way but one, she amended silently. Discounting the quite fantastic physical chemistry, surely marriage needed more than liking and friendship to make it work?

'Well?' he demanded. 'Is the idea of marriage to me complete anathema, Ellis?'

'No,' she admitted, clearing her throat. 'Just—surprising.'

'Why so surprising? You must know how I enjoy your company. Lord knows I'm never off my knees, begging you to grant me some of it!'

She smiled shakily. 'Come off it, Matt, that's a bit much. I just can't picture you on your knees in any circumstances. Besides, when you first brought the subject up I didn't realise you meant marriage.'

'Ah, yes,' he said very softly. He moved closer. 'That's right, you didn't.'

Ellis eyed the gleam in his eye with misgiving, and shifted away until she was jammed up against the arm of the sofa.

'In fact,' Matt went on, a thoroughly unnerving look on his face, 'in response to what you imagined I was suggesting you said you wouldn't hesitate, if it weren't for your career!'

She turned her head away sharply. 'That was different,' she muttered.

Matt slid his arm behind her, turning her face to his with his free hand. 'Why?'

'I—I was being polite. You know how it is. Letting you down lightly,' she improvised wildly, her eyes sliding away from his.

Matt shook his head reprovingly. 'You're suffering from Pinocchio syndrome again. For shame!' He slid his fingers into her hair, holding her head immobile as he looked into her eyes. 'Tell the truth. If, career and Colcraft apart, you wouldn't hesitate to set up house with me, Miss Worth, why won't you say yes just as promptly to a proposal of a far more permanent kind?'

'I suppose,' Ellis said slowly, 'because for me marriage would have to be just that—permanent.'

'I agree wholeheartedly. Which is why I firmly believe that a marriage based on what *we* have going for us has infinitely more chance of success than an alliance based on pure emotion!'

'Will you give me time to think about it?'

His eyes shuttered. 'Of course.' He released her and moved away.

Ellis sighed. 'You're offended.'

He shook his head. 'No, I'm not offended. In fact I'd have been surprised if you'd given me an answer immediately.'

'It's not for some whim, or because I need to talk it over with anyone, Matt. I just need time to get used to the idea.'

Matt eyed her quizzically. 'All right. It's not long to Christmas. I want your answer by then. I'd prefer it sooner, of course, but I'm a reasonable man, Miss Worth.'

She laughed. 'As long as things go the way you want, Mr Canning!'

'When's this blasted exam of yours?' he asked suddenly.

Ellis pulled a face. 'Wednesday.'

'Right.' Matt jumped to his feet, pulling her up with him. 'I'll leave you in peace until then, but, proposal or not, I expect a lot more of your time once you've taken your nose out of your law books.' He took her in his arms and kissed her very thoroughly, leaving her breathless and flushed as he raised his head. 'A thought to take to bed with you, Ellis. Once my heart is set on something I never give up.'

Ellis leaned back against his linked hands, her eyes quizzical. 'You mean your mind, Matt, not your heart!'

*   *   *

Ellis had arranged to take three days off to prepare for her law exam, glad to be out of Matt's vicinity for a while as she crammed feverishly in preparation. She'd said nothing to her mother or Lydia about the proposal, feeling there'd be time enough for that if she decided to accept. Which, she admitted secretly, she probably would. Only a fool would turn down the chance of marrying a man like Matt, with security, a beautiful home, and encouragement of her own career as icing on the cake. And, Ellis thought wryly, except where Charles Longman was concerned, she was certainly no fool.

The exam went well. Ellis sailed through it without a hitch, pleased she'd proved to herself, more than the lecturer, that the subject was no longer a problem for her. When she emerged from the college with a crowd of fellow students Matt was waiting for her.

'Well?' he demanded, neatly detaching her from the rest. 'How did it go?'

'Very smoothly!' She smiled at him radiantly. 'How nice of you to meet me, Matt.'

'I came prepared to celebrate—or commiserate, as the occasion dictated,' he chuckled, as he led her towards the Lotus. 'I assume you walked here tonight, despite my instructions to the contrary?'

'I like the exercise before class. It stimulates the little grey cells—but I was going to take a taxi home,' she assured him.

'I'll believe you.' He slid into the driving seat beside her, then leaned towards her, turning her face towards his so he could kiss her. 'I've missed you, Ellis.'

Her heart missed a beat. 'I've missed you, too,' she whispered, then chuckled. 'I'm starving, Matt.'

'Right. Where shall we eat?' he asked, starting the car.

'Let's call at my local Chinese and take home stacks of fattening things and have a picnic!'

'You're on!'

Later, when Ellis professed herself too replete to move, Matt helped her gather up the foil dishes strewn about her sitting-room, took turns with her in the bathroom to wash away all traces of their feast, then pulled her down on the sofa beside him with a sigh.

Ellis lay against him, utterly relaxed. 'That was fun,' she said drowsily.

'I agree.' He rubbed his cheek over her hair. 'By the way, I hope you haven't forgotten the company Christmas thrash this weekend, Miss Worth.'

'No fear.' She twisted round to look up at him. 'I bought a new dress for it ages ago.'

'If you gave me an answer to my proposal right now,' he said swiftly, 'I could announce it on Saturday.'

'What if my answer's no?'

For answer he pulled her to him and began to make love to her with an air of purpose which soon had her in a state of mind where she was ready to say yes to his proposal and anything else in the world he wanted.

'That's coercion,' she gasped at last, pushing him away. 'You said you'd give me until Christmas.'

'I was a fool!' he said bitterly, his mouth stifling her protests as he pushed aside her sweater to caress breasts already taut and expectant from his love-making. Ellis clutched at him wildly, her nails stabbing him through his shirt, and suddenly Matt scooped her up in his arms and strode with her into the bedroom. He laid her down on the bed, then leaned over her, a hand either side her head, his eyes dark and imperious.

'I want my answer now, Ellis.'

Ellis stared up at him, filled with a strange feeling of destiny. Deep down she'd known, hoped even, that this would happen when she suggested they came back here to the flat. It was all part of the night, of her euphoria over her exam, her delight at finding him waiting for her afterwards, of the laughter they'd shared as they wolfed the meal cross-legged on the floor together.

'Perhaps,' he said very softly, 'I should help you make up your mind.'

Ellis clenched her teeth to stop them chattering as he undressed her very slowly, his eyes caressing each curve as his fingers, sure and skilful tonight, took infinite pleasure in their task. She bit hard on her lower lip, helpless to control the response of her body to the almost tactile caress of his eyes. Her breasts grew taut, her nipples hardened, and Matt breathed in sharply, then stripped off his clothes, never taking his eyes from her until they were in each other's arms. The contact of their naked bodies was like a match to tinder, touching off a blaze which dispensed with all preliminaries, fusing them together in a union so sudden and total and all-consuming that Ellis discovered for the first time what it meant to become one flesh.

They lay entwined and motionless afterwards for a long time in the quiet room, Ellis still clutching Matt's hair as his head lay heavy between her breasts. At long last he raised his face to look into her eyes, taking in a deep, unsteady breath.

'Are you still undecided?' he whispered.

She smiled slowly, her eyelids still heavy. 'Is that why you——?'

'You know damn well it wasn't. For once in my life, Ellis, I was out of control.'

'As persuasion it was very powerful!'

'It wasn't intended that way.' He touched a hand to her tousled hair. 'At that particular moment I'm afraid I wasn't thinking about persuasion, or anything at all except how much I wanted you.'

Suddenly Ellis realised she was desperately tired. She struggled to fight back a yawn. 'Sorry, Matt. Believe me, I'm not bored—just tired all of a sudden. It's been a big night. A very big night,' she added, smiling at him as he released her with flattering reluctance.

'I'll take myself home and let you get some rest.' He eyed her moodily as he pulled on his clothes rather more slowly than he'd taken them off. 'I wish you were coming with me. After tonight,' he added militantly, sitting on the bed beside her, 'I won't leave you in peace until you give in.'

'Why?' she asked calmly.

'*Why?*' Matt pulled her up against him, shaking her a little. 'Because I want you with me all the time, Ellis, not just a few snatched minutes now and then—and *not* just because I want to make love to you. There's a lot more to marriage than that—and I want it all. With you.' He kissed her lingeringly, as though he meant to leave her with the impression of his mouth on hers long after he was gone.

'All right,' she said shakily, when he raised his head.

Matt frowned. 'Does that mean what I think it means?'

She nodded. 'It means yes, I'll marry you.'

As his eyes lit with victory she held up a warning hand.

'On one condition, Matt.'

He groaned. 'I might have known. What is it?'

'That we keep it to ourselves until after Christmas. We'll tell my mother then, and announce it to the world in general in January, when we get back to work. If that's all right with you,' she added belatedly.

Matt shook her hard. 'Is that *all*? I thought you were going to make me sweat out some trial period, or some other torture you'd thought up for me.'

'Your opinion of me isn't very flattering, Matt Canning!' She pushed him away indignantly, reaching for her dressing-gown.

Matt caught her in his arms. 'If I stayed to tell you the exact nature of my opinion where you're concerned, Ellis Worth, I'd never get home tonight.'

Matt, fortunately for his own peace of mind, he told Ellis when he rang her the following evening, was away for the following two days. 'I find myself wanting to tell all and sundry how lucky I am. Won't you change your mind and let me announce it on Saturday?'

Ellis, deeply flattered, almost gave in for a moment, glad she was on the other end of a telephone line rather than in his arms. 'No, Matt. I want to enjoy the dance, and I won't if I'm the object of everyone's attention.'

'I'm going to have a hell of a job trying to hide the fact that you're the sole object of mine! What are you doing right now?'

'Having an early night,' she said sedately. 'I didn't sleep much last night, one way or another.'

He sighed, 'Neither did I,' then proceeded to tell her very graphically how much he wanted to be with her right that very minute, and what would happen if he were.

'Stop, stop,' she implored at last, 'or I won't sleep tonight either.'

'That makes two of us. What time shall I call for you on Saturday?'

After which a lengthy argument ensued because Ellis was immovable on the subject of coming alone to the Chesterton in a taxi. Arriving in company with the managing director was no part of her plan. 'Not until we make it official, after Christmas,' she said firmly.

'Can I at least expect a dance with you?' he demanded. 'Or is dancing with the managing director against the rules, too!'

Ellis's eyes grew dreamy at the thought of floating round the floor with Matt in her new, rather spectacular ballgown. 'I'd love to dance with you,' she assured him, 'but you'll have to dance with all the other wives too.'

'Other wives?' he said silkily. 'Does that mean you think of yourself as my wife already, Ellis?'

Ellis blushed, unseen. After the night before it was something she didn't find difficult at all.

The silence was so prolonged that Ellis thought they'd been cut off before Matt said very huskily, 'Ellis, if I get back early enough tomorrow night, I'll be round on the way home.'

Ellis bit her lip. 'Oh, Matt, I won't be here! I promised I'd go straight to Briar Cottage after work to pick up my dress. My mother's shortening it for me. I said I'd stay the night and come back here on Saturday morning.' She hesitated. 'But I cancelled the usual Sunday lunch. I kept the day free to spend with you—if you like.'

Matt expressed his approval of the idea in such forthright terms that it took Ellis hours to get to sleep once she'd put down the phone.

When Ellis was finally ready for the Colcraft dinner-dance she knew she'd never looked better in her life. The dress, in heavy caramel satin, left her shoulders bare, the skirt a sweeping, two-tiered affair which, according to Polly Worth, made her daughter look like a princess. Ellis fastened her amber chain round her neck, then cast a last critical glance at her eyes and face, both of which glowed with such radiance that she smiled at her reflection happily.

'You look like a woman in love!' she told herself, then stood, transfixed, gazing into her blank green eyes in the mirror as the truth dawned on her. She'd been so blind! All the high-flown talk of friendship was so much nonsense in her own case—she'd been in love with Matt for weeks without knowing it. The revelation sent colour flooding into her cheeks. She swallowed, blinking. Of course it was true. Other-wise, she realised, the scales suddenly falling from her eyes, she would never have said yes when Matt asked her to marry him.

When Ellis arrived at the Chesterton she was touched to find Godfrey in the foyer, waiting for her.

'My dear!' he said, standing back to look at her after he'd taken her wrap. 'How did you arrive—by fairy coach? You look quite dazzling, Ellis.'

She swept him a curtsy, smiling affectionately. 'I've ordered the pumpkin for midnight to take me home!'

Godfrey tucked her hand through his arm. 'You're late, Ellis. Matt's been restive. I'm detailed off to look after you.' He gave her a smug little smile. 'A bit eld-erly for Prince Charming, of course. No doubt someone will usurp my role later. In the meantime come and greet Matt, as is his due, then I shall escort you to a table.'

The room was already packed with a laughing, animated crowd very plainly out to enjoy themselves, the ladies a blur of rainbow colours against the black tie sobriety of the men. Ellis returned greetings and smiles on all sides as Godfrey led her through the crowd towards Matt, who detached himself, smiling, from the knot of people clustered round him the moment he caught sight of the newcomers. He paused in front of Ellis, his eyes sweeping over her from head to toe. He held out his hand, and Ellis, her heart giving a wayward leap beneath the satin at the brief contact, gave him a composed smile as she greeted him.

'Good evening.' He smiled, his eyes holding hers. 'You look sensational! Godfrey, get Ellis a drink, then show her to the table. I'll be with you as soon as the last stragglers arrive.'

'Don't be too long, dear boy, I'm hungry,' sighed Godfrey. 'They can't serve dinner until you give them the green light.'

Sarah, in charge of the seating arrangements, had been annoyingly mysterious, hinting that Mr Canning had departed a little from the Colcraft norm. When Godfrey finally installed her in her place Ellis found her table companions were Dan and Rose Hennessy, a bright young man called Tom Driscoll from marketing, Sarah, smiling conspiratorially, and Vicky, wide-eyed and dazed as she found herself seated between her own boss and the managing director, who slid into his seat opposite Ellis, apologising for holding everyone up.

'I've been hanging on for some late-comers,' he announced, signalling to the head-waiter, 'but I've given them up.' He raised his glass. 'Merry Christmas, everyone, and a successful and profit-making New Year!'

The toast echoed round the room, as the democratic mix of employees at every table set out to enjoy the evening to the full.

They were halfway through the first course when Ellis, who was seated with her back to the entrance, saw Matt's eyes narrow across the centrepiece of poinsettias when a slight pause in the chatter heralded the appearance of two people Ellis had been praying would stay away. She turned, resigned, to see the Longmans heading across the floor. Clarissa, in layers of chiffon the exact ice-blue of her eyes, made a beeline for Matt to make apologies for their lateness, bestowing rather blank smiles on the rest of the table as she registered his unusual assortment of dinner partners.

Charles muttered something perfunctory to Matt, then detached his wife firmly. He halted as he passed Ellis, an oddly bleak quality in his smile as he greeted her briefly before installing Clarissa at the next table among a group of juniors from the department her husband had once headed.

The buzz of conversation resumed and intensified all round the room, and Ellis, after a swift, communing look with Matt, went on with her meal with an appetite sharpened by the fact that she'd felt no reaction of any kind at the sight of Charles. She joined in the general conversation and laughter with such high spirits that she intercepted a questioning look from Matt at one point, and smiled at him radiantly, not even caring if her feelings for him were there in her eyes for Matt and everyone in the world to see. Suddenly she wanted to share her happiness, wishing now she'd let Matt announce their engagement tonight, as he'd wanted.

When the meal was over and the small band struck up for the first dance, there were some surprised faces when, instead of one of the latest hits from the top ten, the strains of a waltz filled the air.

Matt rose to his feet, and Ellis tensed. Surely he didn't mean to sweep her out on an empty floor in front of the entire Colcraft workforce! Matt, however, had different ideas. Smiling at the curious faces on all sides he walked to a table on the far side of the room and bowed to an elderly lady, who rose to her feet in astonishment. There were cheers as the tall, tawny-haired man began to revolve with the small, plump figure in a bright blue dress, and Ellis watched with a lump in her throat.

'Who on earth is that?' asked Rose Hennessy in wonder, and, on learning it was one of the cleaners who kept the Colcraft building so immaculate, clapped her hands in warm approval, then jumped to her feet, beckoning to everyone to join the couple on the floor.

The success of the evening was assured from that moment on. Ellis danced every dance, with partners who ranged from Godfrey for that first waltz right down to the newest recruit in the accounts department. The evening was half over before Matt, who had danced with every other lady at the table first, took her on to the floor. He held her tightly, his hand just brushing the bare skin above the low back of her dress.

'At last,' he said, his lips barely moving. 'Will you blush if I say I could eat you? You look edible in that dress.'

'You like it?' she asked demurely.

'You know damn well I do. So does every other man in the room.' He looked down at her broodingly. 'Longman more than anyone else, by the way he can't take his eyes off you.'

Because the music was the slow, smoochy variety, the lights were low enough for Ellis to risk a smile which made him breathe in sharply.

'I hadn't noticed,' she said, holding his eyes very deliberately.

His arm tightened about her, then relaxed again. 'I'm taking you home, Ellis,' he stated brusquely.

'Right now?'

Matt missed a step. 'I wish I could—why didn't you let me announce our engagement tonight? Then I could have danced with you for the rest of the night if nothing else.'

Ellis tightened her hand on his, in full agreement with him by this time. 'I wish I had now, Matt. But I haven't told my mother yet, so we'd better keep to the original arrangement.'

Matt abandoned her with some reluctance when the music stopped, his face suddenly inscrutable as Charles sauntered up to ask Ellis for the next dance. Ellis resumed the floor with her new partner with some reluctance, unsurprised to find that Charles, the expert at social graces, was a much better dancer than Matt.

'You look utterly ravishing,' Charles said, staring down her as he guided her skilfully across the floor.

'Thank you.' Ellis smiled politely. 'So does your wife.' Which was true. Clarissa passed by at that moment, laughing up into Dan Hennessy's face, looking quite breathtaking.

Charles eyed his wife's graceful back with malevolence. 'Do you think so?' He turned away deliberately, then went on to question Ellis about her new job, asking rather wistfully if she missed him.

Ellis assured him brightly that of course she did, rather embarrassed to find that it was some time since she'd thought of Charles very much at all, let alone missed him. She was relieved when she was able to leave Charles for the excited chatter of Vicky Fisher, who by this time had forgotten any shyness, and was having the time of her life. Suddenly Ellis yearned for a moment of solitude and slipped away to the small cloakroom on the first floor.

It was pleasant to be alone, away from the noise and music for a little while, but after only a moment or two her privacy was invaded by the last woman in the world Ellis had any desire to see.

'I saw you sneaking off, Ellis,' said Clarissa Longman, yawning. 'Lord, but I hate this sort of thing! I couldn't see the point under the circumstances but Charles insisted we came.'

'You look very well, Mrs Longman,' said Ellis, closing her small gold purse with a click.

Clarissa looked her up and down. 'So do you, my dear—positively blooming. I watched you dancing with Matt.' Her eyes glittered coldly. 'I could tell at a glance you languish no longer for poor dear Charles. But then, power like Matt's is so aphrodisiac, isn't it?'

'I really must go, Mrs Longman——'

'Why so formal, darling? Besides, I want you to know I'm very pleased for you.' Clarissa's smile was feline. 'After all, I was the fairy godmother who begged Matt to keep you on at Colcraft, you know.'

Ellis halted, her hand on the door-handle. She turned to face her tormentor, feeling as though all the blood were draining from her veins. 'No. I didn't know.'

'Oh, dear, have I put my foot in it?' Clarissa shrugged in mock apology. 'I asked Matt to hang on to you as a favour to me, to draw your fire, so to speak. Of course at the time I was convinced you and Charles were lovers.'

Ellis stared at her in cold distaste. 'I was your husband's secretary, nothing more.'

'Oh, come on, admit it!' said the other woman scornfully. 'Weren't you just a teensy weensy bit in love with Charles?'

'I was fond of him, yes,' admitted Ellis stiffly. 'But only within the confines of a business relationship.'

'What a stuffy creature you are, to be sure. Not that it matters now, anyway,' added Clarissa carelessly. 'I made a bet with Matt that he couldn't make you fall in love with him instead, and, of course, as it would with any red-blooded male animal, it put him on his mettle. He assured me he'd have you eating out of his hand in no time.' She sighed impatiently. 'Which was a waste of time, as it turned out, because it wasn't you at all, but that cat Monica Caldwell. Matt needn't have bothered.' Her blue eyes gleamed with malice. 'On the other hand it stopped you running after Charles to get a job at CCS. I thought it was high time you realised he belonged to me.'

'Really?' said Ellis calmly. 'I thought he didn't any more.' She walked to the door, then turned. 'By the way, are you citing Mrs Caldwell as co-respondent in the divorce?'

'Oh, I've given up the idea of a divorce!' Clarissa hesitated artistically. 'You might as well know, I suppose. I'm pregnant. Oh, not by Charles,' she added quickly. 'I decided to play my darling husband at his own game. I took a lover. Unfortunately he's married to someone else and wants to remain that way, the swine. So the baby will be brought up as Charles's child.'

'He agreed with that?' said Ellis, horrified.

Charles Longman, it appeared, had no real choice. 'I'm the one with the money, my dear! Besides,' said Clarissa, her eyes sparkling, 'I held the final trump card. When he jibbed a bit at first I threatened to broadcast the reason why I'd never got pregnant before. Charles, you see, just doesn't have what it takes to make babies!'

CHAPTER TEN

ELLIS held up her skirt with both hands as she tiptoed down the wide staircase, doing her best to avoid Charles, who was pacing up and down in the foyer, looking at his watch.

'I say, Ellis, are you all right?' he asked, catching sight of her. 'You look ghastly!'

She tried to smile, wondering if her face was as pale as it felt. 'I do feel rather off. Must have eaten something.'

He eyed her with concern. 'Look, I'll drive you home. I can come back for Clarissa. I'll leave a message at the desk.'

'No—please!' After what she'd just heard Ellis found it hard to look Charles in the eye. She shook her head vehemently. 'Just get me a taxi...'

'Rubbish! You're not fit to go home alone,' said Charles firmly, and marched her through the main doors, his hand under her elbow. Ellis shivered as Charles hustled her swiftly across the frosty car park. 'You must be coming down with flu,' he said, frowning, as he bundled her into his car. 'Are you still in Sycamore Road?'

Ellis barely heard him, her mind still reeling with Clarissa's revelations. With every turn of the wheel she sank deeper into misery, her teeth chattering as it dawned on her that her present job, with its built-in promise of promotion, was probably all part of Matt's master plan to keep her away from Charles at any price. She swallowed on a sudden surge of nausea.

Had the price included making love to her to win his bet?

When the car drew up outside the flat Charles helped her out carefully, looking down into her face with concern. 'Make yourself a hot drink and get to bed, Ellis; you look positively ropey.' He sighed heavily. 'I miss you quite a lot—you always provided such a sympathetic ear for my troubles.' The yellow light from the street lamp gave Charles's handsome face a jaundiced, haunted look. 'Clarissa's pregnant, you know.'

Ellis nodded numbly. 'I know. She told me just now.'

Charles stiffened, a look of mortification dawning in his eyes. 'Did she tell you——?' He stopped, taking in a deep, shaky breath. 'I can see she did. Bloody funny, really, isn't it?' He tried to laugh. 'You disapproved of the way I fooled around so much, didn't you, Ellis? I only did it because Clarissa was so wrapped up in her bloody horses she never had time for me. Now she's turned the tables with a vengeance—and I just can't cope!'

Ellis felt a sharp pang of pity. 'Oh, Charles——' She reached out a hand to touch his cheek, and with a choked sound he drew her to him in a sudden urge for comfort, both of them so fathoms deep in their own disparate misery that neither heard the Lotus until it braked to a halt a short distance away. With a gasp Ellis thrust Charles away in sheer panic as Matt burst from the car and punched Charles on the nose all in one movement.

'Matt, for heaven's sake!' said Clarissa irritably, hugging her fur coat about her as she got out of the car. 'There was no need for that, you idiot!'

Charles backed away from the murder in Matt's eyes, utterly flabbergasted. 'What the hell——?' He put a hand to his nose in horror. 'I'm bleeding!'

Matt started after him, his face black with menace. 'Keep away from Ellis in future or you'll get a damn sight more than a nosebleed, Longman.'

'So sorry, Ellis!' said Clarissa. 'I merely mentioned Charles had taken you home, you know. I never dreamed Matt would get so melodramatic about it.'

'Didn't you?' Ellis eyed her with contempt, by this time so cold in her satin dress that all she wanted in life was to get indoors to some warmth. 'I must go in. I'm freezing. Goodnight.' She set off for her stairs at a run, shaking off Matt's hand violently as he caught her halfway up, but he seized her by the elbow, dragging her the rest of the way without ceremony. He snatched the key from her shaking hand, unlocked the door and thrust her inside into her own sitting-room.

Ellis turned on him like an avenging fury, her skirt swirling in the small space, brushing a cushion to the floor. 'Get out of my flat, Matt Canning!'

He clenched his fists, his eyes glittering with rage. 'What the hell's got into you? I thought Clarissa was lying when she said you'd gone off with Charles. Am I supposed to believe this poppycock about feeling ill?'

'*You*'re angry with *me*! That's rich!' Ellis flung away to her bedroom, slamming the door in Matt's face.

'Come out of there, Ellis!' he thundered, ''or I'll break the bloody door down!'

'Oh, be quiet! I have neighbours, remember.' She marched out, hugging an ancient cardigan round her, careless of its incongruity over the satin ballgown. 'I happen to be cold. I left my wrap behind.'

'Too blasted eager to run off with Longman, I suppose!'

Ellis brushed past him to the kitchen to fill a kettle. 'Don't be so idiotic.' She spooned coffee into a mug with a shaking hand. 'Charles just happened to be standing there as I ran away after a little encounter with Clarissa. He offered to take me home, so I went. If King Kong had offered I'd have gone just the same!' She turned to find him suddenly still, his face haggard beneath the bright hair. 'That's shut you up rather effectively, I see. Is it possible you can guess the gist of Clarissa's little discourse in the powder-room?'

Matt took the mug from her and slammed it down, imprisoning her against the kitchen counter with a hand either side of her. He lowered his face to within inches of hers. 'What exactly did she say, Ellis?'

'Clarissa Longman made it very clear that you kept me on at Colcraft at her specific request,' said Ellis bitterly. 'At the time, of course, she thought I was Charles's bit on the side. An opinion you obviously shared. So for old times' sake you did as she asked, assuring her that you'd have me eating out of your hand in no time. Not, of course,' she added scathingly, 'that you lost out by it. I'm a damned good secretary.' She moved restively, but he remained immovable, keeping her prisoner. 'If you won't let me go perhaps you'll answer a question instead, Matt Canning!'

'What do you want to know?'

'*Did* you make a bet with Clarissa?'

His face set in harsh lines. 'In a way, but——'

'Then there's no more to be said.' Her eyes glittered with unshed tears in the pallor of her face, and with sudden, superhuman effort, she pushed him aside and made for the other room. 'If you hurry,' she flung over her shoulder, 'you can get back for the last waltz.'

Matt swore under his breath and tried to catch her back against him, but Ellis dodged out of reach, her face rigid with distaste.

Matt dropped his hands. 'Just *listen* to me for a moment!' he said through his teeth.

'What's the point? I've already heard more than enough.' Ellis went to the door and held it open, shivering in the cold blast of night air. 'Just go—*please*!'

He strode through the door, then turned to look at her. 'Is that it? What about tomorrow?'

She stared at him incredulously. 'Tomorrow!'

'Yes. Sunday. We were going to spend the day together.'

'You can't be serious! After what I found out to-night I can't bear to be in the same room with you right this minute, let alone spend an entire day with you. You seem to be missing the point, Matthew Canning. I know now why you set out to—to attract me. All right, you succeeded. I admit it. You won your bet.' She threw her head back, her eyes flashing green fire. 'Did Clarissa stipulate getting me to bed as part of it?'

Matt went white as his shirt. Without warning he pulled her into his arms, crushing her mouth with his, then he put her away from him so suddenly that Ellis staggered as he flung away from her into the cold night.

Since Ellis's disappearance from the Christmas dance had been explained as being caused by a sudden in-disposition, she was almost grateful when fate sup-ported her story by giving her the worst cold she'd ever had in her life. She huddled in bed, shivering and burning simultaneously all that long, miserable Sunday, feeling so ill that only a combination of willpower and pride forced her to drag herself out of bed and off to work to arrive in her office only a little later than usual on the Monday morning.

'I heard you were unwell,' observed Godfrey, eyeing her as he came in. 'I didn't realise you were dying.'

'It's only a cold,' said Ellis, coughing.

'Which,' said Godfrey flatly, 'I would prefer you to keep to yourself. So go home, go to bed and get rid of it.'

Ellis flatly refused, saying she had far too much to do, whereupon Godfrey shut himself in his office and refused to communicate with her other than by telephone, since, he informed her with asperity, he had no intention of ruining his Christmas by catching her germs because she was too pig-headed to stay at home for a day or two. Before the morning was over Ellis felt so ghastly that she would have sold her soul to take his advice. But she remained stubbornly at her post for the simple reason she was sure Matt would attribute the wrong reasons to her absence if she went home. Not, Ellis found, that she saw Matt that day. She knew very well he was in the building. But any communication he made with Godfrey was done through Sarah. Not that she wanted to see or to speak to him, Ellis assured herself fiercely. But the day was longer than any other Monday she'd endured before, particularly since she remained at her desk during her lunch-hour, not only unwilling to unleash her germs on the cafeteria, but unable to face any form of sustenance other than countless cups of coffee.

'Let me bring something up for you!' urged Sarah, calling in on her way to lunch, but Ellis waved her away, shuddering.

'Nothing, thanks. Go away, do, before you catch my cold.'

Godfrey put his foot down late in the afternoon, and told Ellis to get herself home to bed and to stay there for a day. 'It may have slipped your mind, Ellis, dear, but Christmas is almost upon us. If you go on as you are you'll be too ill to enjoy it.'

Ellis knew he was right. She agreed to take the next day off, but promised to return well before Colcraft closed for the Christmas break. As she hurried across the car park she felt rather better. Now she could stay home with honour, since Matt would know by this time from Sarah that a common or garden cold, rather than a broken heart, was the reason for her absence. Ellis returned to work on Wednesday, heavy-eyed and pink-nosed, but to the casual observer a lot more like herself. Godfrey, satisfied she was convalescent, welcomed her back, overwhelmed her with paperwork, then left her to her own devices for the rest of the morning while he attended a meeting chaired by the managing director in the boardroom. Sarah, taking advantage of Matt's absence, came to drink her mid-morning coffee with Ellis.

After a brief discussion of the dance, and enquiries about Ellis's health, Sarah said casually, 'By the way, when I told Mr Canning how ill you were on Monday he looked *very* concerned.'

'Probably afraid I won't finish my stint on the pension proposals,' said Ellis without turning a hair.

'Rubbish!' Sarah turned in the doorway. '*I* think—and Vicky agrees with me—that there's more to your relationship with our sexy managing director than you let on, Ellis Worth.'

'You couldn't be more wrong,' Ellis informed her sharply.

One of Sarah's eyebrows rose. 'I see—you're just good friends!'

'You're wrong about that, too, so beat it, Sarah Lewis, and let me make up for the time I've lost.'

Determined to clear her desk by Christmas, Ellis went on working for over an hour after Godfrey's departure that evening. At last she stretched wearily, pushing her spectacles up into her hair. She put folders away in her desk drawer and locked it, then sat very still, sensing she had company. She turned slowly, her heartbeat choking her at the sight of Matt standing tall and formidable in the doorway, his eyes scrutinising her colourless face.

'I heard you were ill,' he said.

'Just a cold.' Ellis took her raincoat from a cupboard, keeping the desk between them as she belted the coat, her fingers clumsy with the discovery that she badly wanted to throw herself in his arms and cry on his shoulder. 'It's late,' she said wearily as she crossed the room. 'I must get home.'

'If you've been ill, why the devil didn't you go home hours ago?' he demanded, barring her exit.

'I wanted to make up for the time I've lost.'

Matt's eyes held hers. 'So you're going to stay in the job?'

'Of course. Why shouldn't I?'

'After the events of Saturday night I thought you might find the air of Colcraft too contaminated by my presence to remain here.'

She gave him a scathing look. 'Certainly not. Only a fool allows personal feelings to interfere with career prospects.'

Matt stepped aside, ushering her into the corridor. 'I see. My mistake—one of the many I've made where you're concerned.' He shrugged. 'I suppose I might as well make one more. I came here to ask you to listen to my side of Clarissa Longman's story.'

Ellis wavered, sorely tempted for a moment. Then she hardened her resolve. 'It really doesn't matter,' she assured him casually. 'As far as I'm concerned it's all water under the bridge. Goodnight.' And with a friendly little smile she walked away down the corridor, feeling his eyes like a burn between her shoulderblades until the lift doors closed behind her. Reaction set in once she was alone. When she reached the ground floor Ellis abandoned any pretence of calm and flew outside into the damp, cold night, racing towards her car as though the devil were after her.

During the time left before the holiday Ellis met Matt in passing on more than one occasion, but there was no further exchange between them other than a polite greeting. Which was the way she wanted it, Ellis assured herself firmly, and blamed her cold for the depression which resulted in bitter tears now and again for what might have been. She wished she could postpone Christmas altogether until some other, happier year. With no heart for the task, she went shopping for gifts in the stores which kept open late in the evenings of Christmas week. Recorded carol music blared at her as she pushed her way through the shoppers who thronged the centre of Pennington. The familiar strains merely added to her depression, and she cursed Matt Canning for getting under her skin to the stage where life had no savour or point without him.

Ellis had arranged to arrive at Briar Cottage during the afternoon of Christmas Eve, certain that in her current disorganised state the morning would be needed for last-minute shopping. She longed for the festivities to be over, dreading the final day at Colcraft, when a turkey lunch was traditionally served in the cafeteria to all members of the company, management included, for this one special occasion. It was an effort to join in the fun when she knew very well that Matthew Canning, from his vantage point at the head of the management table, had an excellent view of Miss Ellis Worth pushing her subsidised lunch round her plate.

'Time you started eating again,' commented Vicky. 'That cold really pulled you down.'

Ellis smiled. 'Don't worry—a few days of Briar Cottage cuisine and I'll soon be back to normal.'

Sarah and Vicky exchanged a look.

'We do worry,' said Sarah, under cover of the general noise. 'Because it isn't just the cold, is it?'

Ellis looked away. 'I've been working hard as well, I admit. But a week or so off and I'll be fine— promise.'

It seemed like years before she could make her escape back to her office. As usual at Colcraft everyone went home straight after lunch, and when Godfrey Baker was ready to leave he handed Ellis a brightly wrapped package, kissed her cheek and told her to forget about work for a week.

'It'll all be waiting here for you when you get back,' he pointed out.

Ellis smiled at him affectionately, exclaimed with pleasure over the tortoiseshell fountain pen he'd given her, then handed over a gift-wrapped book on sea-fishing. After he'd gone she tidied his office, then her own, lingering over the task in the forlorn hope that Matt might call in to see her before he left. When it became depressingly clear he had no such intention, she put on her coat, gathered up her belongings and made for the lift, her forbearance tried to the limit when she found a knot of young men waiting in ambush when she emerged into the foyer. With a wild war-whoop they charged towards her, brandishing a clump of mistletoe. With no way of avoiding them Ellis submitted as cheerfully as possible to their bois-terous attentions, only to find herself released so abruptly that she almost fell into the arms of the managing director, who, it was plain to all concerned, was not amused.

'That's enough, you lot,' he said, not unkindly. 'Time to go. Merry Christmas.'

'Time I went home too,' said Ellis briskly, as Matt held the heavy glass door open for her.

'Are you spending Christmas with your mother?' he asked, as they walked across the car park.

She nodded brightly. 'Yes. I'm off there tomorrow afternoon. And you? Are you off to Devon?'

'No, not this year.'

'Merry Christmas, then,' she said quickly, longing to ask him how and where he *was* spending the holiday.

When they reached her car Matt stood looking down at her for a moment, then stepped back, raising his hand in salute. 'Merry Christmas, Ellis.'

Ellis drove into Pennington through a haze of tears, which proved a great nuisance while she was trying to find a place to park. She mopped herself up vig-orously, then set off to do some last-minute shopping requested by her mother. Afterwards she went through her own Christmas list with such unexpected ease that she was home long before dark. She made herself a pot of strong black coffee, then settled down on the floor in the sitting-room to wrap her gifts, pleased to find her favourite Christmas film on television. But for once *Meet Me In St Louis* was a bad choice. By the time Judy Garland was halfway through 'Have yourself a merry little Christmas', Ellis had to mop herself up for the second time that day, and gave herself a sharp ticking-off for being such a misery.

An hour or so later, with nothing left to do, Ellis decided it was pointless to hang on at the flat, alone and miserable, when she could be with her mother and Lydia. There was no answer when she rang to tell them she was coming, which was no surprise. Her mother and aunt were always inundated with invitations at Christmas time. They could be anywhere. She'd get there first and surprise them, Ellis decided, feeling a lot more cheerful. She had a quick bath, put on a bright pink sweater and comfortable old cords, added flat leather boots and an ancient suede jacket, then stowed her presents in a holdall, collected her suitcase and the carrier-bag of shopping for her mother. On her way to the car Ellis called in on the elderly couple on the floor below to wish them the compliments of the season, then set off for Briar Cottage with the firm intention of enjoying her Christmas in spite of Matt Canning.

As usual at that time of night, Christmas or no Christmas, there was no traffic once she'd turned off on the narrow minor road which led to Briar Cottage. Ellis drove along at her usual moderate speed, feeling so much better by this time that she could hardly believe it when three miles short of her destination disaster struck. The car began to make sinister spluttering noises before slowing down inexorably, and eventually, to Ellis's utter dismay, it stopped dead. She gave a wail of horror, then switched off the lights to save the battery, plunging the road into instant, Stygian darkness.

Oh, boy, she thought. What now? She made several attempts to restart the car, but with no success. She took a torch from the glove compartment, pulled the lever to release the bonnet and got out to investigate. Ellis shone the light on the jumble of machinery without hope. It looked pretty much as it always looked—incomprehensible. She stared at the engine malevolently, then banged the bonnet shut. Even if by some miracle she discovered what was wrong she had no way of putting it right. She would just have to walk the rest of the way to Briar Cottage.

She disliked the idea of locking her belongings in the boot. There was nothing for it—she'd just have to lug everything home. The likelihood of a lift was pretty remote on this road. It was long past the time when breadwinners were driving home to their loved ones, and no one would be out joyriding on a cold December night. Ellis stuffed her handbag into the holdall, then set off with suitcase in one hand and holdall and carrier-bag in the other, with no free hand for the torch. To her shame she soon found out she was very nervous in the darkness, which seemed menacing now she was out alone in it, instead of bowling along in her car.

After a while the bags began to feel very heavy. Her eyes soon became accustomed to the darkness, but a chilly wind rustled eerily in the trees, and there were strange, unidentifiable scufflings in the hedgerows.

Ellis gave herself a stern lecture, telling herself not to be such an idiot. If only she could walk faster! But the bags seemed to grow heavier with every step, slowing her to a snail's pace. Ellis ground her teeth in frustration, furious with herself for not keeping to her original plan. Her mother wasn't even expecting her tonight, so no one knew where she was. If I'm murdered out here in the back of beyond, she thought in sudden panic, no one will know I'm missing for ages. She broke into a run at the thought, then forced herself to slow down. She had a long way to go. There was no point in wearing herself out. After Christmas I'll join a keep-fit class, she vowed, panting, mortified to find herself in such poor shape. Suddenly her heart leapt. A car was coming! As lights swept into view round a bend she darted out into the middle of the road to flag the car down, but in her eagerness lost her footing and with a scream tumbled over, her various bits of luggage landing on top of her as the car screeched to a halt a short distance away. She lay winded for a moment, gasping as a torch shone in her eyes.

'*Ellis?* What the hell are you doing?' Matt hauled her to her feet with ungentle hands.

Ellis, giddy with relief, could have kicked her rescuer as he set her on her feet. 'Practising for the London marathon!' she snapped, brushing herself down. 'You nearly ran over me,' she accused.

'Rubbish!' Matt kept an iron grip on her elbow as he shone the torch over her head to foot, then released her to stow her scattered belongings in the back of the Lotus. 'I wasn't anywhere near.' He turned back to her, seizing her in his arms. 'I saw your car back there—what the blazes happened?'

'It stopped,' said Ellis succinctly, half of her so glad to see him that she wanted to throw her arms round his neck and smother him with gratitude, the other half angry at being discovered in such a ridiculous situation.

Matt bundled her in the car, then strode round to get in the driver's seat. 'I ascertained that much for myself,' he said with sarcasm. '*Why* did it stop?'

Ellis shrugged angrily. 'How should I know? It just did. It wasn't my idea to get marooned miles from anywhere with all this stuff, I assure you.'

Matt breathed in deeply. 'Have you thought what could have happened? You could have been assaulted, robbed——'

'Oh, shut up, Matt!' she cried, incensed. 'Do you imagine I wasn't afraid of that? I thought of a few other things, too, believe me. My imagination's been running riot every step of the way. I've never walked along here in the dark before.'

Matt cursed under his breath and ordered her to take better care of her car in future to avoid anything similar happening again.

Ellis's indignant retort was forgotten as she discovered Matt had just taken the turning into Rectory Lane. 'I would like,' she said very coldly, 'to be driven to Briar Cottage, if it's not too much trouble.'

He shrugged. 'Not much point at the moment. No one's in. Your mother's gone to a carol concert with your aunt.'

Ellis stared at him, dumbfounded. 'How do you know that?'

'I had tea with them this afternoon,' he said casually as they reached the house. 'Come in and have a drink. I'll take you home later.'

She scrambled from the car to follow him. 'Matt, don't be so infuriating—what on earth were you doing at Briar Cottage, for heaven's sake?'

Matt opened the door and ushered her into the hall. 'First things first,' he said implacably. 'Run upstairs and wash the mud off your face, then come down and have a drink while I explain.'

Ellis eyed herself in horror when she reached the bathroom. There were dead leaves caught in her hair, which looked like a bird's nest above her dirt-streaked face. She made hasty use of one of Matt's combs, washed off the dirt, then went back downstairs, too curious about his visit to Briar Cottage to care much what she looked like.

Matt was leaning against the chimneypiece, gazing down into the fire he'd just lit. He looked up with a smile as she joined him. 'What can I offer you? Brandy, gin, wine?'

Ellis accepted a glass of wine, her eyebrows raised when she found the glass contained vintage champagne.

'It is Christmas,' Matt said, shrugging. 'My first in my new home. I felt we should mark the occasion.'

'Compliments of the season,' said Ellis rather perfunctorily. 'Now *please* tell me what you were doing at Briar Cottage.'

Matt settled himself a discreet distance from her on the sofa. 'I went to enlist your mother's aid, and your aunt's too, with a problem I have.'

'I fail to see how they could be of any help to *you*!'

'On the contrary.' He eyed her over his glass. 'Because you're the problem, Ellis Worth, your mother seemed the best person to ask for help with a solution.'

She eyed him militantly, her eyes flashing. 'You had a nerve!'

'I think you've forgotten something very important, Ellis.' He smiled significantly. 'Once I've set my heart on something I never give up. I told your mother that this afternoon when I asked her advice on the best way to get you to listen to me.'

Ellis, secretly deliriously happy to hear it, stared at him truculently, in no way prepared to make things easier for him just yet. 'And what did she say, may I ask?'

Polly Worth, not in the least put out to find the managing director of Colcraft Holdings on her doorstep, had introduced him to Lydia, plied him with tea and mince-pies and listened to what he had to say without interruption.

'I like your mother enormously,' said Matt, smiling. 'Your aunt I found a little formidable at first, but when she realised my intentions were of the best she began to thaw.'

'Well, tell me what you had to say!'

'I told them I wanted to marry you. So I told my story from start to finish, without embellishment.' Matt looked her in the eye. 'The truth, incidentally. Not Clarissa Longman's version.'

Ellis, wishing she'd been a fly on the wall at Briar Cottage that afternoon, eyed him thoughtfully. 'I see. Perhaps you'd better tell me, too.'

'Ah, but will you believe me?' he said swiftly.

'If it really is the truth, yes.'

Matt drained his glass and set it down, turning to relieve Ellis of hers. He moved closer, sliding his arm along the back of the sofa as he began to explain, in the concise, lucid way she was used to from many a board meeting, that Clarissa Longman had asked him as a personal favour to keep Charles's secretary on at

Colcraft, to prevent Ellis from following Charles to CCS.

'As if I'd have done anything so stupid!' said Ellis in disgust. 'Anyway, did you agree?'

'Yes.' Matt met the fire in her eyes unmoved. 'But I had a reason.'

She frowned. 'What reason?'

'Unknown to her, Clarissa was preaching to the converted.'

Her eyes narrowed. 'What do you mean?'

'When you passed me in the car park that morning there was such zest and enthusiasm in every line of you. You made for that building as if it were Mecca—I couldn't take my eyes off you. I was so curious to know who you were that I asked a discreet question or two at reception a few minutes later.' He shook his head. 'When I heard you worked for Longman I could hardly believe my luck. I assumed you'd automatically come to work for me once he was gone—it seemed like fate.'

'When you came across me mid-embrace with Charles didn't you change your mind?' she said drily.

'No. I arrived on the scene *before* the kiss, such as it was. Your obvious amazement made it clear it wasn't a regular occurrence. Besides...' Matt moved closer, an unnerving gleam in his eye. 'I was confident I could make you forget Charles Longman pretty quickly once he was out of the way.'

Ellis nodded, resigned. 'Eating out of your hand in no time.'

His eyes narrowed. 'Do I hear quotation marks?'

'Clarissa's phrase.'

Matt breathed in deeply, then leaned forward, his face only inches from hers. 'Ellis, listen. Those were her words, not mine. Clarissa did ask me to keep you at Colcraft, and she did make some kind of stupid bet about how fast I could make you fall in love with me. But the point is, my darling, that I was already firmly committed to both plans long before that. And solely for my own sake, not hers.'

Ellis turned away, her eyes on the flames leaping in the fireplace. 'You never said anything to *me* about falling in love, Matt.'

'No,' he said shortly. 'You know my views on that subject. I wouldn't let myself use the word "love". I persuaded myself that what we had together was respect, friendship, tastes in common. I explained this to your mother.' He reached out a hand to hers and clasped it tightly. 'But I didn't shock her by mentioning the chemistry between us.'

Ellis turned to look at him, an odd little smile twitching the corners of her mouth. 'Mother probably took that for granted!'

He grinned. 'When I told her about punching Charles on the nose——'

'You did what?'

'I was explaining why you wouldn't speak to me.'

'Charles's nose has nothing to do with it.'

'Your mother thought it was highly significant.'

'Did she? And after all this catharsis of yours did she provide you with the solution you were after?'

Matt rubbed a long forefinger to and fro on the back of her hand, smiling a little. 'In a way. She looked me in the eye and told me the remedy was in my own hands, that I should be laying my case before the daughter, not the mother. Which was such sound advice that I immediately took off to Pennington to act on it, only to find the bird had flown.'

'What would your next move have been?' asked Ellis, her eyes on the hypnotic stroking finger.

'I've already made it.' On finding her gone Matt had consulted her neighbours, learned she was on her way to Briar Cottage and set off after her in hot pursuit. 'Can you imagine what I felt like when I found your empty car? I went berserk. It took only a minute or two to find you, but it seemed like a lifetime.' He pulled her into his arms, holding her close as he rubbed his cheek over her hair. 'I was off my head picturing what might have happened to you, afraid I might never have the chance to say my piece.'

'You've got the chance now,' she said huskily.

'I just wanted to tell you I love you.' He smiled, elated, as he tipped her face up to his. 'Amazing! It's so easy to say, after all, when it's to the right one. Lord, what a blind fool I've been! All that poppy-cock about friendship went out of the window when I found you with Charles after the dance. I was so raving mad with jealousy that he's lucky it was only his nose which suffered. I wanted to kill him.'

Ellis pulled a face. 'He's got enough on his plate without that.'

'To hell with Charles,' he said roughly, and shook her a little. 'Well?'

Ellis looked away, feeling suddenly awkward.

He shook her slightly. 'Since I've never made a declaration of love before, is it unreasonable to expect some kind of response?'

'No,' she admitted gruffly.

'It's possible my instinct was wrong, of course,' he said softly. 'Maybe you don't love me after all.'

'Of course I love you!' she said irritably. 'I wasn't the one rabbiting on about friendship, Matt Canning—you were!'

He let out an explosive sigh of relief, then began making love to her with a new possessiveness which made it very easy indeed for Ellis to tell him, very disjointedly between kisses, how desperately she loved him, and how miserable she'd been and how much she'd hated the idea of Christmas until tonight.

Since Matt's responses to these confessions were everything, and more, that Ellis could have wished for, it was some time before any normal conversation was resumed. Held tightly in Matt's arms, her head on his shoulder, Ellis's mind turned at last to practicalities. 'Shall I ask Mother to invite you to Briar Cottage for Christmas dinner?'

'She already has, darling.'

Ellis threw her head back, hooting at the smug triumph on his face. 'What if we hadn't made it up?'

Matt's grin widened. 'No chance of that! My pride was at stake. Your mother put me on my mettle by hinting that if I really didn't know the best way to bring you round perhaps I wasn't the right husband for her daughter after all.'

Ellis groaned. 'I must have a word with my lady mother!'

Matt glanced at his watch, sighing. 'You'll be able to have it quite soon, I'm sad to say. She wants you home tonight, sweetheart, and I'm to make sure you get there.'

'I don't want to move, Matt,' she whispered.

He kissed her lingeringly, stroking her hair back from her forehead. 'Neither do I. To be very honest, Miss Ellis Worth, all I want in the world at this moment is to take you off to bed and make love to you all night. But I promised your mother I'd get you home early, so I shall.' He ran a probing finger over her bottom lip, his eyes holding hers. 'But be warned. My restraint is unlikely to prove so absolute in future.'

'I'm happy to hear it,' she said candidly, smiling as she pushed herself to her feet. 'Heigh-ho, let's go home to my darlings, then, and get them off their tenterhooks. The carol service must be over by now, and, by the way, I'm starving. You may have plied me with champagne, Mr Canning, but you haven't given me so much as a crumb to eat.'

'Your aunt's putting on supper for us both at Briar Cottage,' he said, throwing up a hand like a fencer at the look on her face.

'My goodness,' said Ellis tartly. 'You were sure of me, weren't you?'

Matt seized her hands, suddenly in deadly earnest. 'That's just the point, my darling. I wasn't. After the look of loathing you turned on me that night I was afraid you'd never let me near you again.'

'Oh, darling!' She moved into his arms, hugging him close. 'It wasn't loathing. I was just so—so *hurt*! What a stupid, stupid fool I was for believing Clarissa Longman.' She looked up at him. 'She must really hate me, Matt.'

He shook his head, looking grim. 'It wasn't you she was aiming at, Ellis. It was me. Once, in the dim, distant past, Clarissa decided it would be fun to take me away from her friend Laura. I told her to get lost in no uncertain terms, and she took it rather badly. She's waited a long time to take her revenge, but she succeeded in the end.'

'Oh, no, she didn't!' said Ellis, eyes sparkling.

Matt's eyebrows rose. 'You're right—as usual. The success was all mine, after all.'

'Mine too!' she reminded him, then gasped, her eyes wide with sudden dismay.

'What is it?' he asked sharply.

'I'd forgotten about my car! What can I do about it, Matt?'

He hesitated, rubbing his nose with a long finger. 'Ellis—now don't hit me, but just exactly when did you last fill up with petrol?'

Ellis flushed guiltily, her eyes flickering. 'Well—er—I can't quite remember...'

'Now, then—own up!'

She let out a wail. 'Oh, Matt, I'm such an idiot, I meant to fill up this afternoon, but I was so tired and miserable, I just forgot.'

Matt shook with sudden laughter. 'Well, well, so the infallible Miss Worth makes mistakes after all, just like the rest of us.'

'You want perfection?' she demanded crossly.

'No. I want you. Just the way you are—warts and all.'

'I don't have any warts!'

'I know, my darling, I know.'

Their eyes met in sudden, charged silence.

Matt cleared his throat. 'We'd better go. My good resolutions are crumbling fast. Come on. We'll put a can of petrol in the Lotus, rescue your car, then I'll drive right on your tail all the way to Briar Cottage.' He paused, searching in his pocket on the way to the door.

Ellis laughed. 'I suppose you're dead keen to show Mother and Lydia how easy it was to smooth me round—oh!' she gasped, her eyes like saucers as Matt slid a ring on her finger.

'*Easy!* If your car hadn't broken down we'd probably still be arguing the toss—does that fit?' he added casually.

Ellis stared speechlessly at the band of emeralds on her finger. 'It's—it's glorious,' she said faintly, and threw her arms round his neck to kiss him over and over again.

'I had that in my pocket at the Christmas dance,' Matt said unevenly at last. 'I was all set to put it on your finger when I took you home, but things went badly wrong, didn't they? So wrong I was afraid for a while they'd never be right again.'

Ellis hugged him close, her eyes glistening with happy, unshed tears as she smiled up into his face. 'Yet it was so simple to put it right in the end, wasn't it?'

Matt smiled teasingly. 'You mean all I had to do was load you with jewels?'

Her eyes shone green for danger for a moment, then filled with a different, softer light. 'No, Matt Canning. All you ever had to do was say you love me!'

HARLEQUIN PRESENTS®

is

- ☑ exotic
- ☑ dramatic
- ☑ sensual
- ☑ exciting
- ☑ contemporary
- ☑ a fast, involving read
- ☑ terrific!!

*Harlequin Presents—
passionate romances
around the world!*